Future
History
2050

Future History 2050

Written by **Thomas Harding**

Graphics by Florian Toperngpong

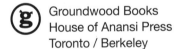

Groundwood Books
House of Anansi Press
Toronto / Berkeley

Groundwood Books / House of Anansi Press
groundwoodbooks.com

Groundwood Books respectfully acknowledges that the land on which we operate is the
Traditional Territory of many Nations, including the Anishinabeg, the Wendat and the
Haudenosaunee. It is also the Treaty Lands of the Mississaugas of the Credit.

We gratefully acknowledge the Government of Canada for their financial support of
our publishing program.

With the participation of the Government of Canada | Canadä
Avec la participation du gouvernement du Canada

Library and Archives Canada Cataloguing in Publication
Title: Future history 2050 / by Thomas Harding.
Other titles: Future history two thousand fifty. | Future history twenty fifty.
Names: Harding, Thomas, author.
Description: Previously published as German translation: Berlin: Verlagshaus
Jacoby & Stuart GmbH, 2020.
Identifiers: Canadiana (print) 20210236558 | Canadiana (ebook) 20210236639 |
ISBN 9781773068039 (hardcover) | ISBN 9781773068046 (EPUB)
Classification: LCC PS3608.A7345 F88 2022 | DDC j813/.6—dc23

Jacket design by Michael Solomon
Fire photo: REUTERS / Alamy Stock Photo
Printed and bound in Canada

Groundwood Books is a Global Certified Accessible™ (GCA by Benetech) publisher.
An ebook version of this book that meets stringent accessibility standards is available to
students and readers with print disabilities.

Groundwood Books is committed to protecting our natural environment. This book
is made of material from well-managed FSC®-certified forests, recycled materials, and
other controlled sources.

MIX
Paper from
responsible sources
FSC® C016245

For Moo. Incredible. — TH

A brief message from the researcher

Honestly, I didn't know what to make of it.

I was in the Landesarchiv in Berlin doing research. It is an old armaments factory to the north of the city, a large red brick building with high ceilings and polished floors. On a small table in front of me were seven cardboard boxes. I had already been through three of them, finding much of interest about a Jewish family who lived in Berlin in the 1930s. It was particularly interesting as one of the boxes contained letters from the Gestapo.

I then opened the fourth box, and that's when I found them. A stack of nine notebooks, each filled with handwritten notes. They were numbered 1, 2, 4, 6, 7, 9, 10, 11 and 13. The calligraphy was neat and, surprisingly, given where I was sitting, in English.

I looked more carefully and noticed several dates. On the front page of the notebook in my hand was written 2031. I flipped forward a few pages and saw the year 2033. And then, at the back, 2035.

My interest now piqued, I looked at the other notebooks. The dates ranged from 2020 at the start of one to 2050 at the back of another. Then, as I was moving through the pages, a document fell out. It was a postcard from somebody who had fled Venice after dramatic sea-level rise had flooded the city.

It was dated 2031. But how could this be? That was almost eleven years into the future.

Having spent years examining documents in windowless rooms around the world — some call me an archive rat — I am by nature skeptical. But I am also a man of reason. My training is to investigate the facts in front of me without prejudgment or bias.

So, after a deep breath, I lifted the document for a closer look. Certainly, it appeared original, neither a copy nor a facsimile. The postcard itself seemed authentic. The document's wear and tear appeared real enough. The signature at the bottom, though ornate and hurried, looked original.

My heartbeat was now racing. I told myself to be calm. To be analytical. Perhaps this was someone's effort at science fiction and it had been left here in error. But if so, surely they would have returned to the archive to collect it once they realized they had lost their precious property.

Alternatively, and more likely, this was a prank. A fellow researcher's attempt at tricking her or his colleagues. But this, too, I quickly ruled out. Would someone really go to the trouble of writing this lengthy history as a joke? By my quick calculation the notebooks contained more than two hundred pages. Faking these documents would be an enormous and highly difficult task. And the consequences of discovery would be draconian. That left one option. That this was real.

Which was unthinkable. Absurd. Even if this was a true history written by some person in the future, how had the material found its way back to 2020? I had heard, of course, about time travel. And I'd read articles about wormholes and irregularities in the space-time continuum. But that was the stuff of novels and movies. Entertaining for sure, but nonsense to a scholar such as me.

And yet, what if this was real?

I had nothing pressing to do that day. I would read these notebooks carefully, cataloging any inconsistencies or issues I found as I went along. This was the task I set myself: if by the final page I believed that the artifacts — I was, I must confess, already giving these notebooks the respect of such a name — were more likely real than not, I would have to conclude, as a professional researcher, that the notebooks were indeed a future history.

I began reading the first notebook and, to my profound surprise the more I read the more I believed. I soon noticed numerous gaps in the narrative. Entire years were missing. I also observed that the Interviewer and the Historian, if that is what they were to be called, focused on just one, or at most, two events per year. No explanation was given.

So here they are. I present these notebooks as I first found them, including the various artifacts that were slipped in between the pages, and starting with an introduction from the Interviewer. I have made no attempt to edit or redact. Best, I believe, to make available this remarkable account, including any flaws and omissions, as I first discovered it. As to its veracity, I leave it to you, dear reader, to decide.

Thomas Harding
January 2020

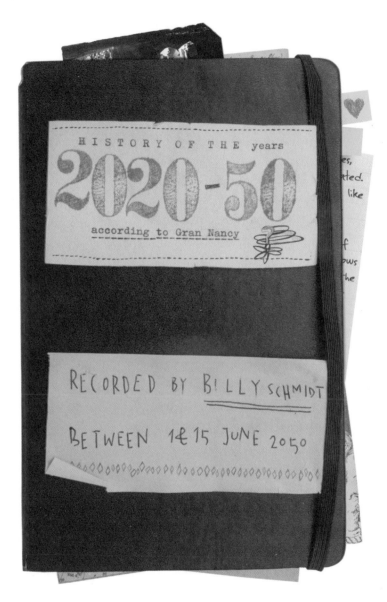

HISTORY OF THE years
2020-50
according to Gran Nancy

RECORDED BY BILLY SCHMIDT

BETWEEN 1 & 15 JUNE 2050

Notebook 1

About Me

Gran Nancy says that all history is personal. I agree with that. History is real, it happens to people and, if you look carefully, you can see traces of it in their day-to-day lives.

Sure, it is thrilling to read about how and why wars start and end, how monarchs lost their thrones, how a brilliant scientist invented some fantastic machine, or an artist created a totally new form of expression. But to me, the everyday is just as interesting. Perhaps even more. What did people eat and drink? What did they wear? How did they spend their time? What did they talk about? Who did they fear? Who did they love? What made them get up in the morning?

So in the spirit of history being personal, here is a little about me.

My name is Billy Schmidt. I am fourteen and eleven months. I live in London with my parents, two older siblings and my gran Nancy. My home is small but it's enough for the six of us. We live in a city tower, with 25,000 neighbors. Everything's in the tower, near where we live: shops, a gym, a town square. Everything is 100 percent recycled.

Here is my typical day. I wake up at 9:15 a.m. to the sound of breakfast being prepared by Cook930. Most days I have a piece of fruit (grown in the local mega-greenhouse) and a carb-bar (rice or soy). School starts at 10:00 a.m. I can't believe that when my parents went to school they had to start at 8:00 a.m. or even earlier. My brain hardly functions at 10:00!

After lunch, I do my Community. At the moment, this has me reading stories at the local elementary school. Most of the classes are given by roboteachers, which are great in that they can individualize the lessons. Having said that, humans can obviously give something that robots can't provide. Humor for one. Physical touch for another. I enjoy spending time with the little kids. I'm thinking of working in education administration when I'm older. But that's years off. First, I have to finish my mandatory years of education and then three years of public service. By then I'll be twenty-seven years old.

After school, my friends and I go to the gym. My best day is Wednesdays, as the bike I've been allocated is next to the window and I get to look at the Biodiversity Restricted Area outside the city. On Fridays, my friends and I love to go to the giant city cinemas.

In the evening, my family goes to the public cantina for dinner. It is located just a few floors down from where we live. If I have exercised well, I treat myself to dessert. My favorite is to have one of the new Insta-ices. These only became available last year, and I love that I can design the flavor, texture and shape. (Last night my Insta-ice looked like my cousin. I laughed when I bit off the nose!) We're usually back home by 11:00 p.m.

Then I watch a show for an hour or so. My current obsession is a detective series set in 2010, where the justice department relies upon human detectives to catch the bad guys. I yell out when they miss the obvious clues. And when the police detectives walk into a crime scene without a protective forensic suit, that makes me laugh! What were they thinking? They will obviously contaminate the crime scene. Ah, the good old days!

My one great desire is to play football for the All Stars. My coach says I'm good enough, but that I have to work harder in practice.

My other dream is to travel. We're limited to the flood-free zones, but there are still plenty of attractive destinations. But it's expensive to leave the city tower. The energy required to complete even a short journey is extreme — and that's just ground transportation. My parents and gran talk about flying on airplanes, but I've never been on one. No one my age has. They were outlawed back in 2029 at the height of the CLIMATE SHOCK. There's a lot of talk about inventing a carbon-free means of mass air travel, but the technology hasn't been invented yet.

This year we plan to go on a week-long trip to Edinburgh. One day, I hope to travel to the Alps. I'm told there is still one glacier remaining. I would love to see that. And the wildflowers are meant to be spectacular, at least that is what my friend Katia says.

I was born on July 5, 2035. My first memory is

blowing out four candles on a birthday cake. It was a medieval castle. The crenulations were made of chocolate with orange and yellow candy on top. To be honest, I don't know if I actually remember this or if the memory comes from the picture my parents took. Either way, I look happy, with long shaggy hair and a big smile on my face.

Apparently I did not start talking till I was three and a half. My parents say that I have been making up for it ever since. I'm the youngest of the family and another of my early memories is my siblings yelling at me, "Stop asking so many questions!"

Medieval castles are one of the things I know a lot about. I've read all the books I can find on them. I can tell the difference between a motte and bailey (wooden and on a hill), a stone castle (made of stone obviously) and a concentric castle (lots of inner walls and courtyards). I can tell you about the things the defenders used to chuck at the attackers (molten tar must have really hurt) and the contraptions used by the attackers (ladders, battering rams and catapults). For example, did you know that crenellations are made up of crenels, the open spaces through which you fire arrows that are the width of an outstretched arm, and two merlons, the solid wall between two crenels?

I love everything from the past. In addition to castles, my favorite subjects are the dinosaurs, the Romans and the Han dynasty in China. I am particularly interested in how each of these kept huge power for a long time, and then lost it.

So yes, I'm obsessed with the past. My favorite hobby is reading history books. My parents say that as soon as I could read, I never went anywhere without my Library 1500. I loved that thing!

I kept having to expand my storage. At eight years old I was given five iShelves. I needed fifteen by the time I was ten, and forty-five by thirteen. One iShelf can hold one hundred books, so that is a lot of books! Some people erase their iShelves to make way for new books. I kept them all.

But books and watching old movies can only take you so far. Best of all is hearing it direct from those who witnessed history taking place. And so, whenever I have the time, and as long as my gran doesn't run out of energy, we hang out and chat about the old times. We talk and talk and before I know it, two or three hours have gone by. For someone who is 102 years old, Gran has an excellent memory.

This week, I've decided to interview Gran Nancy properly and will start taking notes. I have always kept a personal journal, keeping track of what I do each day on my All-in-One: what I'm reading, the big events (if any) of the day.

But this is different. This is about history and I wanted the record to be correct. I told my calligraphy roboteacher I wanted to practice my handwriting at home. The next day, two packs of paper notebooks arrived at our door along with three pencils.

Gran Nancy was pleased about the notebooks.

"Biographers have always relied upon handwritten letters and typed documents," my gran said. "I wonder how historians will find out about people today given everything is only on social media?"

Gran Nancy is always doing this. Taking a small point and blowing it up into a life lesson. Usually I don't mind, but sometimes I find it annoying. Like today. So I spoke my mind.

Gran Nancy smiled and shrugged. "You know what they say: you can't teach old dogs new tricks."

I rolled my eyes.

When we sat down for our first formal interview, Gran Nancy said that there was one condition — I must take everything down "verbatim." When I asked what that meant, my gran shuffled slowly over to a huge trunk, opened the lid, reached in and lifted out a large blue block, before shuffling slowly back holding the object tight.

"This is for you," Gran Nancy said, dropping the block in my arms. It was heavy!

Looking closer I saw that the block was actually a battered navy blue cardboard case containing two large printed books from the old days. It was a paper dictionary and it was enormous! Above the books was a little drawer. This contained a large magnifying glass.

As Gran sat down, I did a quick search about the dictionary on my All-in-One. Apparently, the dictionary was first published in 1928 in twelve volumes and took more than seventy years to complete. Amazingly, it contains 414,800 words. That's a lot of words. The people who made the dictionary must have realized that most people don't have space for twelve volumes in their homes. So in 1971 they republished it as two volumes, with the entries shrunk to make them fit.

"Take out P to Z," Gran Nancy said. I did what I was told and flipped to V for verbatim. The letters were unbelievably tiny. I have good eyes, but this was impossible to read. My gran told me to use the magnifying glass. I started looking for the right page.

Ventriloquist. Venture. Verbalize. Verbatim.

The book said that verbatim comes from the Latin *verbum*, or word, and means "word for word" or the "exact words."

Apparently, the first record of verbatim being used in print was in 1481 in the city of Coventry in England and had something to do with King Stodealf.

I was looking up King Stodealf on my All-in-One, and finding nothing, when my gran said, "If language is what sets us apart from other animals, that book provides the keys to our species. It's yours."

This is another thing Gran Nancy does, give me old things. Actually, I like this. My room is filled with really cool stuff. I've got a typewriter, a vintage doctor's bag (with a real stethoscope and sewing kit), a letter opener and an abacus.

"So," Gran Nancy said, "do you promise to write everything down verbatim? Even if you think it's boring or you don't like what I say?"

I promised.

Gran Nancy looked at me hard like I didn't mean it.

"I promise," I said and stared right back. This time I really did mean it.

Gran Nancy then said — and this was very exciting — that as we went through the years Gran would give me various objects, like letters, pictures and other memorabilia. That made me excited. Besides history being personal, I've also been taught that reliable history needs supporting evidence.

Gran Nancy next asked which period of history I wanted to know about. When I said the time that affected my life, my gran suggested we go fifteen years before I was born and fifteen years after, to the present day.

So here are Gran Nancy's recollections of the past thirty years.

2020

Is your All-in-One recording?

Okay, let's begin with 2020. It's a good year to start.

2020 was when I stopped giving regular lectures to the students. I had been a professor of sixteenth-century English history at Cambridge University for thirty-five years. I loved teaching, but I was looking forward to more time for myself. I had just been commissioned to write a book. So, 2020 was the end of one chapter — forgive the pun — and the start of another.

I used the money from the book advance to purchase a new car. It was my first driverless vehicle. It was a marvel! It could park by itself. It could change lanes by itself. On one journey, I had too much fun using the driverless mode and the car told me off.

"Place your hands on the steering wheel!" it yelled. "Place your hands on the steering wheel!" The car wouldn't let me use the driverless function for the next 300 miles.

Just the year before, the first pedestrian had been killed by a driverless car. It was very sad. And it demonstrated that the path to an automated future was not without its perils.

2020 was also the year that we were told for the first time that it was too late to stop the planet from warming. That we had crossed a line. That significant climate change would happen no matter what we did.

We still had a choice, however. If we made radical changes to our society, and made them soon, we could limit the impact of climate change. We would still feel the effects, but we could adapt quite easily.

But if we did nothing and ignored all the dire warnings, the consequences would be catastrophic. Sea-level rise. Floods. Plagues. Mass species extinction. Crop failure. Hurricanes and tornadoes. Life as we knew it would be destroyed. Our future, they said, would be hopeless.

We therefore had to choose between a bad future and a really bad future.

I remember this time well, as I was hard at work, writing my book on climate politics. I stayed up late researching the latest scientific studies. Writing about recent history is not easy as there is not enough distance to see things in their proper context. When I did read the news, I first looked for anything about the climate, and then I read the sports results. I rarely had time to look at anything else in great detail.

I do remember a few other events.

A royal baby was born.

A TV show about a man who kept tigers in cages was popular.

I think it was about then that for the first time, a private company sent a rocket to the International Space

Station — at that time, space missions were still launched from the Earth. The country that used to be called the United Kingdom exited the European Union. A trade war erupted between the superpowers China and the USA. And a terrible virus spread around the world, killing millions of people and causing economic and social havoc.

At the time, all these events appeared to be of great consequence. Now, incredibly, none of these happenings are well remembered. Even the greatest disasters are forgotten, replaced in our memories by a more recent crisis, and then the next. They are time's flotsam and jetsam. As a historian, it is important to identify what is significant rather than what is attracting the most attention. Or, as some say, to separate the wood from the trees.

My Thoughts

I've decided to make some notes as I go. To add my comments and anything interesting I find along the way.

I had no idea that I was living with a history professor. To me, my gran has always been "Gran Nancy," who read us stories when we were young and helps with the household chores. Always around.

Nor did I know that driverless cars were not available for most of Gran Nancy's life. The story about the space station was cool, though I can't believe that space missions were launched from the Earth in the old days. It makes so much more sense that they start from the Moon base.

The bit about climate change sounded like typical Gran Nancy. Always talking about the end of the world and how life was so much better "back in the day." I've learned to look like I'm listening at these moments, but not really listen.

I am going to remind Gran that I want to hear about historical events and to stick to the facts.

2021

I am sticking to the facts!

Amidst all the noise and distraction to be found in the news media of this era, there was one critical moment I wish to record for 2021: it was a massive investment in quantum computing.

At the time, the news attracted little attention. Looking back across three decades, this was a key moment that transformed the world. Scientists had for years been looking for a way to significantly increase the speed of computers. One of the most advanced research centers was in Cambridge. I knew some of the lead scientists and it was through them that I learned of the remarkable, game-changing work taking place at my university.

The science behind the new technology was complicated, which is one of the reasons the media did not cover the story. I asked a friend of mine to explain it to me. I will try and remember what she said.

It went something like this: in theory, a quantum computer is able to figure out algorithms at 100,000,000 times the speed of a traditional computer chip. Traditional computers had until this point relied on circuits with binary values — either one (on) or zero (off). A quantum computer is not limited to this either-or way of thinking. Its memory is made up of quantum bits or qubits. And qubits do both-and — meaning that they can be in a superposition of all possible combinations of zeros and ones; they can be all of those states simultaneously. Add to this another crucial concept of entanglement — which syncs particles separated by vast distances — and then a quantum computer offers massive improvement over traditional computers.

In October 2019, Google announced that it had achieved quantum supremacy — the moment when a quantum computer could perform a task that a traditional computer could not. In the months and years following the announcement, huge investments were made into quantum computing. My friend said that it would be only a matter of time before we saw the impact on our day-to-day lives.

She was right. This technology became the breakout event of the next three decades.

Only a handful of quantum computers have ever been made. They are simply too expensive to build and they consume vast amounts of energy to run. But these very few extraordinary devices have been transformative. One application helped doctors untangle the hugely complex interaction of atoms and molecules in human anatomy, which has led to the discovery of new treatments and medical procedures. Another improved weather forecasting — a notoriously difficult task given the large number of variables — which has become vital to vulnerable communities particularly after the SHOCK.

People also say that these machines are used by the government to monitor all activity on the One/Net. They can search vast databases of images, text and audio, both live and in archive. If this is true, I don't have a problem with it. As my late husband, your gran Jack, used to say: the only people who have anything to fear are those who have something to hide.

Most important of all, the quantum computer was the reason behind the rise of the Ethnarchs.

With this new enormous processing power, these captains of industry were able to gather nearly everything there was to learn about us: what we ate, what we drank, what we liked to watch, what we liked to do with our spare time, who our friends were, what issues were important to us, our dreams, our fears, our secrets.

And with this information, this Mega Data, they provided us with exactly what we wanted, sometimes before we even knew what that was. And they sold us vast amounts of products at affordable prices with efficiency and good humor. Which we loved.

They gave us politicians who promised to solve the issues that mattered to us. And when these politicians failed, we were given others to take their place. All the time, the Ethnarchs became more and more powerful. And the gap between them (a handful of Ethnarchs) and us (the rest of humanity) became colossal, unbridgeable and permanent.

But — and I am being absolutely honest here — I didn't care. Because our lives were better, safer and more fun.

Notebook 2

My Thoughts

Hearing Gran Nancy talk about technology is hilarious. For me quantum computers are completely normal. Gran talks about them like they are some magical tool created by wizards. At the end of the day they're just machines. Humans made them. Nothing to be scared about. The Ethnarchs. Of course, I know all about them as well. Everyone does. They own the world's biggest companies. They run the show. But I didn't know that their rise to power was connected to the quantum computers. I wonder what else I don't know. What other bits of the jigsaw puzzle I'm missing.

After our chat today, Gran Nancy gives me an article from a newspaper called the *Guardian* from 2018. It's printed on real paper, which is cool. I've heard about newspapers of course, but never seen a piece of one before. It's soft to touch. So different than reading words on screen. Weirdly permanent. I can't imagine having to print words and then not being able to change them once they are out in the universe. What a responsibility. How scary! But turns out to be useful, as the information can't be deleted.

I read the article and it really disturbed me. I'd always been told that the SHOCK was inevitable, a part of the "natural order." That there had been long periods of freezing, my teachers said, and now there was a period of warming. Was this wrong?

I went to the library to see if I could find any more newspapers that predicted the SHOCK. At the front desk, I showed Gran's article, and the librarian took a quick look and then disappeared through a swinging door. I scrolled through stories on my All-in-One for thirty minutes. Then, tired of waiting, I sneaked behind the desk and peeked through the window of the swing door. To my surprise, instead of searching through catalogues, the librarian was talking to someone on the phone. I retreated back to the correct side of the front desk before I got caught.

The librarian eventually returned.

"None of the newspapers on file talk about the SHOCK before it happened."

I asked if any other archives would have the missing articles.

"They're not missing," the librarian stammered. "The articles never existed."

Was that a look of fear? The librarian then asked me where I got Gran's article. I mumbled something about finding it in an abandoned house in the forest near the city tower where I live and then left before I had to answer any more questions.

It all happened so fast, but as I walked out of the

library I realized I had not given my name. That at least was a stroke of luck.

Walking home, my mind was whizzing. Someone must have removed the articles from the archives. Were the Ethnarchs trying to hide the fact that they and their companies hadn't done enough to prevent the SHOCK?

I need to ask Gran Nancy about this in our next session. And if there had been an alternative.

The Guardian

Monday
8 October 2018
Issue Nº 53,534
£2.00

Global warming must not exceed 1.5C, landmark UN report warns

Jonathan Watts
Global environment editor

In a stark new warning, the world's leading climate scientists have said that global warming must be kept to a maximum of 1.5C to lessen the risks of drought, floods, extreme heat and poverty for hundreds of millions of people.

The authors of the landmark report by the UN Intergovernmental Panel on Climate Change released today say urgent and unprecedented changes are needed to reach this target, which is affordable and feasible although it lies at the most ambitious end of the Paris agreement's pledge to keep temperature rises between 1.5C and 2C.

The half-degree difference could also prevent corals from being completely eradicated and ease pressure on the Arctic, according to the 1.5C study, which was launched in Incheon, South Korea, after approval at a final plenary of all 195 countries that saw delegates hugging one another, with some in tears.

Inside
'If we act decisively, and innovate and invest wisely, we could avoid the worst impacts of climate change'
Nicholas Stern *Page 13*

"It's a line in the sand and what it says to our species is that this is the moment and we must act now," said Debra Roberts, a co-chair of the working group on impacts. "This is the largest clarion bell from the science community and I hope it mobilises people and dents the mood of complacency."

Huge obstacles remain. Policy makers commissioned the report at the Paris climate talks in 2016, but since then the gap between science and politics has widened. Donald Trump has promised to withdraw the US - the world's biggest source of historical emissions - from the accord.

The world is currently 1C warmer than pre-industrial levels. Following devastating

12 →

2023

There was an alternative.

We could have avoided the most horrendous impacts of climate change, but only if we had made significant changes to the way we lived. We would have had to accept difficult sacrifices. And we would have had to set aside our differences, work together and focus our efforts on building a different society. This would have required enormous effort by all of us: politicians, business people, consumers.

For the first time the option was clear, at least to those willing to listen. We had to choose between bad and cataclysmic.

The shocking thing is that, despite the clear warnings, despite the inevitable result of inaction, despite the obvious need for a change in course, the world went on as if there was no choice to be made.

Though it has been almost thirty years, I am struck by how everything was there to be seen, in plain sight, if people had only looked properly. Sure, there were a few who read the writing on the wall but not as many as you would think. The vast majority kept living the lives they always had, as if there would be no consequences. And if they cared about anything, it was about the issues of the day. Of the now. Who would become president or prime minister. Which sports team would win the next trophy. Whether salaries would be taxed higher. Which celebrity was getting married or endorsing some product the public did not yet know they desperately needed.

The calamities that were to come were either too many years away or too scary for the majority to engage with. The old, typically, did not care as they would not be alive to feel the inevitable consequence of their actions. Some young people did speak up — but mostly they were too preoccupied with getting the most out of each day. And nobody wanted to be lectured. They labeled all concerns as fear-mongering and pushed any thought of future crisis from their minds.

Sure, there were exceptions. Some people changed their day-to-day habits. They drove electric cars, recycled their domestic waste, insulated their homes, reduced their air travel, restricted their nutrition to a plant-based diet. There were campaigners who demanded that governments take significant measures to counter climate change. They were typically young, teenagers or in their early twenties.

I experienced these protests myself.

One day when I was in London, it was around 2018, trying to get to the British Library, my way was blocked by a demonstration taking place on Waterloo Bridge. I wasn't upset. To the contrary, I was pleased. I supported their actions. Amongst their young faces, I saw your auncle Quentin, he liked to attend such protests.

But the vast, vast majority of people on planet Earth did nothing. They made no real changes to their lives. Which was the wrong decision.

Let me get back to the history. Where were we?

Oh, yes, 2023. It was like a violent storm that would eventually turn to sunshine and peace. This perhaps sounds sentimental, but I think it is true.

Looking back, the dramatic shift was perhaps unsurprising. At the time, the violence came as out of the blue. Violence is perhaps too soft a word. Better to speak of it as it truly was — a mauling. Sometimes, it takes one specific moment to change history. This moment was the riot at one of the most notorious prisons in the US. I don't remember the name now, not that it really matters.

I first heard about it online. The prison was one of the largest in the world. Most of the inmates were waiting for trial and had not yet been convicted of a crime. Conditions were terrible. Stabbings and fights were commonplace. Murders happened every month.

The riot started in the canteen, as they often do. Within minutes the facility was in chaos. More than ten officers were brutally attacked, and more than a hundred prisoners were badly injured. Half the prison was on fire. The initial complaint given by the rioters was that the prison was too crowded. Few would have argued with this. The prison was built for 5,000 men, and it was not uncommon for more than 10,000 to be held at the jail on any one day.

Soon, the rioters spoke about other issues. The terrible

food. The violence within the prison. The drugs and the abuse from the officers. The lack of privacy. The depression. The inherent racism in the justice system — in the US, a Black man was ten times more likely to be arrested for a crime than a White man. And worst of all, the lack of hope. For most of them, once released, would soon find themselves back inside this jail, or one similar, as they moved along the conveyor belt of the incarceration system.

What was unusual was that this prison riot spread to other facilities around the country. One prison fell and then another. They seemed to inspire each other. Over the next five years, forty-five prisons, jails and other detention centers were taken over by the prisoners.

When the system was finally brought back under control by the authorities — and after we, the public, had seen years of terrible scenes of destruction and fighting on our news feeds — there was a general outcry for prison reform.

At the time of the riots, the United States had the highest rate of incarceration in the world. While it represented just over 4 percent of the world's population, the US housed around 22 percent of the world's prisoners. Within ten years, the entire system would be transformed. The number of inmates in the US dropped from 2.3 million to just under 200,000. These last were only the most violent prisoners, those who could not be trusted on the streets. The financial savings were enormous and were invested in other government initiatives, including employment projects, to give work to those prisoners now released, and perhaps even more importantly, new ways of producing clean energy.

Other countries soon followed the example of the US. Switzerland, Norway, Brazil, India, China. People were now calling federal penitentiaries and county jails "medieval" and "sadistic," and asking how we — as a civilized society — could have locked people up. Wasn't liberty a basic human right?

By 2035, the world's prison population had halved, and it halved again over the next ten years. But as the prison population declined, we saw security measures increased across the rest of society. Security cameras were now on every corner and the monitoring of our private communications was widespread. Like many others, I was worried about privacy issues, yet I was pleased that the streets were now safer.

But big government decisions like this can have personal consequences, as we shall see.

My Thoughts

This is the first time I've heard Gran Nancy mention Quentin's name. Ever. I am almost fifteen and my gran has never talked about this before. At least not when I'm around.

I said I was glad to hear about Quentin, though it was a little weird because I know next to nothing about my auncle. I don't even know what Quentin looked like.

Later, when I got to my bedpod, I found a paper photograph on my pillow. In the picture, Quentin is a teenager like me. Short hair. Dressed in jeans and a checkered shirt. Staring intensely at the camera, radiating energy. In an instant becoming real. I suddenly realized how strange it is that my family has hidden Quentin's memory.

Then I thought about what Gran Nancy said about the SHOCK. I am so confused. If people knew what would happen, then why didn't they stop it? Just writing that question down makes me feel angry. I wonder what it was like for Gran Nancy to live through it?

Then I think about the prisons. It is hard for me to imagine what life is like locked inside four walls. Why would anyone agree to locking up another human being?

It seems so wrong to me. I am going to see if the library has any old videos of prisons or interviews with prisoners.

These conversations with Gran Nancy are proving even more interesting than my wildest dreams. Wondering what our next session will be about.

Notebook 4

2026

It had been a long time coming, but finally it came. What was it? One word: automation.

We thought it would happen slowly, incrementally, over years. In fact, it took just thirty-six months to revolutionize how we work. It seems that the problem was not technology. That had been solved long ago. The issue was whether the public would accept nonhumans taking over core human jobs. The company bosses and politicians must have got together, taken some polls and made the decision that we were ready. For it didn't rain machines, it poured.

First went the pharmacists. One day I went to the store to pick up some pills and there was a druggist who took your prescription, checked the paperwork, counted your pills and asked if you understood the instructions.

The next time I visited I was speaking to a computer. It was quicker, easier and more reliable. Once the public had accepted this — which they did almost immediately as the cost of everything quickly declined — the flood gates were open.

Within months we saw machines handing out food at

drive-through restaurants. We saw computers giving lectures at schools and universities (much to the relief of the students who could now tailor the education to their needs and interests). Taxis and trucks, trains and buses suddenly drove themselves. Workers such as cleaners and porters, loaders and guards, bank tellers and shop assistants were now replaced by an army of androids and assorted other bots of all shapes, colors and sizes.

And what about all the unemployed humans? Again, the company bosses and politicians had clearly been thinking about this for a long time. Just before the pharmacy owners obtained their licenses to use machines, the government announced that every adult in the country would be guaranteed a place to live and free health care along with what became known as a Dignified Income or DI.

This DI was much more than the previous welfare benefits. Every family now received more than enough to live a good life. They were given enough money to live comfortably, to not only purchase the essentials, but also common luxuries.

Some people asked how we would pay for the DI in the long run. Where would the money come from? Would it not cripple the economy? But the answer was obvious when you thought about it. With machines doing almost all the work, almost no humans had to be paid, so profits were huge. All the government had to do was take a small part of this for taxes and their coffers were full. This wealth was then distributed by the government to the people.

Of course, someone had to be responsible for the machines, for ensuring that they delivered what we needed, what we wanted. Which is why so much money went to their owners, people who started calling themselves the Ethnarchs.

And as automation could only work if it was done globally, money had to be the same everywhere. So, one side effect of DI was the end of national currencies.

I know it sounds strange now, but back then, each country or region had its own money. Japan had the yen. Kenya the shilling. Russia the ruble. Europe the euro. England had the pound. But now there was no need. We had a new currency called the Unified Global Dollar. What we now just call Globals. This made trading between countries so much simpler. No more changing money from one currency to another. When you traveled, your money was accepted everywhere. Life was so much easier!

And there was one other big change. Nowadays we pay for everything with our All-in-Ones. But when I was young, we paid for things using rectangular pieces of paper called "cash" and small metal discs called "coins." Electronic money is so much easier to use. It is also better for the Ethnarchs, who can monitor every single transaction on their quantum computers. This has taken away the opportunity for cheats not to pay their taxes, which means the government has more money to give out. A much better system!

To reassure people about the big move toward

automation, the government paid for a massive publicity campaign. Every day we saw a different advertisement on television, heard a new spot on the radio, walked by a dazzling billboard. The message was as simple as it was exciting. Life was going to be much better after what they were calling the Transition.

The campaign was actually quite funny. Each advertisement was different. They featured celebrities showing how they would now be using their time.

One started with a guy sitting at his desk in a cubicle answering boring telephone calls and tapping away at his keyboard. The next moment he was scuba diving in some exotic location.

In another, a woman was working in a factory one moment, and the next she was staring at a hunky male model in a life drawing class.

A third had a group of young men collecting stinky rubbish, and then suddenly they were having a blast playing video games and eating pizza.

These were super slick videos, each in a different setting, each catering to a different set of tastes and involving a different kind of person: young, old, man, woman, Black, White, Asian. What was there not to like?

In truth, this was not as radical as it first seemed. After all, at the time of the Transition the majority of people were not actually working in paid employment. Children and young adults were in education. Many adults were looking after infants, elderly relatives or engaged in some other unpaid activity. Others were simply part of the long-term unemployed. There were cities in Europe, for instance, where more than 40 percent of young men were unable to find work. Finally, there were those over sixty-five years old who were already retired, and were used to filling their days with unpaid activities.

As for the rest of the population — the eighteen- to sixty-five-year-olds who were employed — most accepted the Transition without a fight. They were typically glad not to work. They now spent their time doing whatever retired people had done up till that point. Fishing and playing tennis. Taking long walks and cycle rides with friends. Watching videos and listening to podcasts. Engaging in the hobby they had an interest in. Attending classes or learning some new skill. Traveling and visiting tourist sites. Sleeping in or going to bed early.

Those who struggled emotionally with the Transition were offered an energy juice that suppressed sad thoughts. There were many flavors produced by a number of companies. The most popular was called Mellow Yellow, a delicious banana and strawberry shake.

Inevitably, there were those who strongly opposed the Transition. Some just liked to be employed. They enjoyed the daily rhythm of going out to a job and returning home after a hard day's work. They liked the social time with their colleagues and being away from their families, especially after all the stay-at-home orders and lockdowns during the recent pandemics. They liked the satisfaction of doing a job well. They found their work stimulating and sometimes even important. They liked the recognition they received from their colleagues and clients. And, of course, they liked the money they received and the independence this gave.

There were also others, many, many others, who thought the new system grossly unfair. The vast majority of the planet now received a fixed income — which, though generous, was capped. This meant that unless you found a way to supplement your income, there was at first no way to improve your family's living standards. Which might have been fine, if everyone was in the same boat.

But they weren't. Because the Ethnarchs, the owners of the corporations and their friends, had become enormously wealthy. They now had as much wealth as a billion other people combined. Some called them The One in a Billions or TOBS. Others called them the Megas. Mega rich. Mega healthy. Mega educated. Mega entertained. Mega traveled. Mega everything.

Finally, there were those who had deeper concerns about the Transition. They worried that with fewer people working, humans would be less creative, less able to develop new fields in the arts and sciences. To this came the reply that we now had robots and computers to work for us, and these were infinitely more hard working, efficient, creative and ambitious. This satisfied most people.

Still, thousands resisted. They said that the Transition took away their self-respect. They said they had been stripped of one of their core liberties — freedom to work. So they marched through the street with banners, shouting slogans such as "Work Gives Us Dignity" and "Fair Pay for an Honest Day's Work."

But by then it was all too late. For it had happened too quickly. The decisions had been made. The actions taken. And just like other great changes in history — when the peasants left the fields and moved to the cities in the eighteenth and nineteenth centuries, or when an increasing number of women took up employment in the twentieth century — the momentum of change was too great for anyone to stop it, let alone slow it down.

By the end of 2026, human employment in Europe and North America had shrunk from 85 percent to 75 percent. Within three years, the number would fall below 60 per cent. And it kept dropping after that, year upon year. This dramatic shift in work patterns was mirrored in Asia, Australasia, Africa and across Latin America. By 2035, and for the first time in their long history, the vast majority of Homo sapiens no longer worked for a living.

There was a dark side to this automation and AI that was kept from us for a long time. Indeed, it may have been the reason for the delayed rollout.

Around the same time as the Great Automation and the Transition, the army was introducing warbots. They were different from the drones and remote-controlled vehicles we had seen before. These new warbots were not flown by remote pilots, they could search for targets by themselves. And they could learn and adapt their behavior. Once they received the command to kill the enemy, the warbots went on a rampage with terrible consequences. They didn't stop until every enemy was dead.

But the enemy had warbots, too.

The result was a series of war crimes that appalled the public. Whole towns were burned to the ground. Civilians were killed in the thousands. And once the warbots realized that a starving enemy was easier to overcome, hundreds of thousands of hectares of crops were destroyed.

When the war crimes cases eventually made it to court, nobody could answer the question of who was responsible: human or machine? While the courts failed to make a ruling, the army ramped up their production of warbots. And the killing of children and the destruction of houses and the burning of crops continued.

Until the summer of 2028, when a secret memo from the Russian intelligence services was leaked to the Western press. Finally, the world saw reason. The warbots had to be controlled. At a summit of heads of state, an international treaty on machine warfare was agreed upon. The treaty was long and detailed, but the most important agreement was that while warbots can harm other warbots, they can never harm humans. Indeed, if a warbot does hurt a human, even by accident, it instantly self-destructs. This command would be hard-wired into every intelligent weapon on the planet.

English translation of a Russian memo
posted on leakforchange.org

GRU_warbot_memo_12-12-28.pdf

GRU
Moscow

12 December 2028

General Schmolski

We are losing the battle against the machines. Despite considerable effort we have been unable to guide their decision-making. Collateral damage continues to be both extensive and disproportionate. Propose immediate rethink of warbot strategy.

Our analysis suggests three alternatives:

1. Invest more resources in defining a protocol that will limit warbots' civilian impact
2. Increase public's tolerance that use of warbots will result in high collateral damage
3. Decommission warbot program

Major Dimitri Andropov

Notebook 6

My Thoughts

I'm a bit grossed out hearing about Gran Nancy and Gran Jack's love life. Does Gran Nancy have to give ALL the details?

I tried asking Gran about Quentin again but once more I got nothing back. It seems that the one conversation was the exception. There's to be no more talking on this subject.

I went to my parents, but they wouldn't say anything more than the usual stuff. "What a lovely person" and "We miss Quentin so much."

But here's the thing. If someone tells me I can't know something, that's like telling me to find out.

So I walked over to Quentin's school — it's the same one I go to and I know some of the people who work in Admin. They said that Quentin was a good student, bright and full of energy, liked by most of the year group. They said Quentin played for The Rugby Team and gave me the names for three of his teammates: Paula, Midge and Benji. They didn't have any contact information, but suggested I reach out to the Alumni association.

I will ask Gran Nancy about The Rugby. Never heard of it.

2028

It's called rugby, Billy, not The Rugby.

Rugby was a very popular sport, particularly in Europe, Australia, New Zealand and South Africa. It was fast-moving and tough. Very, very tough. Both my brothers played, as did my father. They weren't professional, mind, but there was a good amateur league where we lived. When I was older, after I had my children, the people in charge of the sport introduced a long list of technical penalties, which I found confusing and hard to understand. Then came the stories about brain damage, early onset dementia, lower life expectancy.

Which takes us to 2028, the year that the medical community finally put an end to violent sports, including rugby. After years of reports, conferences, memoranda and other delaying tactics, the governing bodies declared that children could no longer play sports that incurred concussion. This immediately ruled out boxing and rugby. It made me sad that other children would not be able to enjoy such sports, but I also worried about people getting hurt. The new laws also ended the NFL, wrestling, skiing and judo. Other sports were permitted, but with restrictions. For example, heading was now banned in football and checking was outlawed in ice hockey.

There were numerous attempts to overturn this decision, but all efforts failed. And without children learning how to play these games, these sports collapsed, with only a few die-hards playing on private property, far away from the media and government eyes.

Speaking of changing values ... let's talk about babies. And in particular, surrogacy.

At first, it was only available to the super-rich. To avoid the physical and emotional hardship that frequently comes with giving birth — the stretch marks, swollen ankles, throwing up, the never-ending discomfort, the pain of labor and, for many, postpartum depression. These super-rich women decided surrogacy was a better option. So they paid other women to carry their babies.

Many said that surrogacy was terrible. Even evil. Especially if the surrogate received payment. Some considered it to be bad for the parents. Without pregnancy, the argument went, they would not bond with their baby. Others worried about the surrogate. Only a desperate person would provide surrogacy, they said, and therefore their rights were likely to be trampled upon.

Rich countries banned surrogacy or made it so difficult legally that the parents were never confident they had custody of their new babies. But this just pushed those looking for a solution to travel abroad. To India, Nepal and Kenya.

For, as is ever the case in human history, laws did not

stop the practice from taking place, they just drove it underground. Gangsters stepped in to the void. Surrogacy became dangerous. Armed criminals patrolled the transactions. Many naive couples were ripped off. A few were devastated after the birth when their baby was kept by the surrogate.

And then there were those who were giving birth. Some were forced by gangs to lend their wombs for profit. These women rarely made any money. Unscrupulous and ill-disciplined doctors were drafted in to oversee the procedure. Hundreds of women died in the backstreets from infection and birth complications.

Eventually, in the mid-2020s, governments regulated the sector. Surrogacy became safe and widely available. A growing number of women learned that they could make good money by providing surrogacy. Others joined in: gay couples who wanted babies, women who were unable to give birth because of medical complications or age, and single people who wanted to have children.

Thus, following the rules of basic supply and demand, a huge market was born. Surrogacy quickly spread in Southern Europe, Singapore, Hong Kong and Australia. More and more people were now taking advantage of what became known as "pain-free birthing." And this was the year that marked this shift. For starting in 2028, one of the Scandinavian countries became the first in the world where a quarter of births were surrogate.

By the time the practice was commonplace, I had long before given birth to my own children, your parent

Robert and your auncle Quentin. The nostalgic part of me misses the old days. The way that biology cut into my life, forced me to slow down, put my body first, set aside my work for a few months. I loved the feeling of having a baby inside of me. The miracle of creating another life. My time of the month, that I don't miss. But luckily for me that stopped years ago.

And here's another shift that I have seen over the years: shopping.

When I was growing up I used to love going to the shops to buy things. I could browse along the clothes rack, try things on and, if I didn't like the material, or the cut, or the price, put it back and leave. I could go to the grocery store or market stall, look at the fruit and vegetables on offer, touch them, smell them, feel the weight in my hand, and if the price was okay, purchase them.

Then came the One/Net (it was called the internet at first) and everything changed. Initially, only certain sectors were affected. First books, then electronics, then food, cars, bicycles. The impact on high streets was slow at first, and then later, brutal. Grocery stores, clothes shops and cobblers came and went, unable to compete with the One/Net. Charity shops selling used items and vintage household goods replaced them, taking advantage of low rent and low taxes offered by the local communities. But eventually even these failed. And soon, high streets were empty. Windows were boarded up.

This pattern happened across the world. England and the US and Canada were the first to change. For a long time, other countries protected their shop owners. They tried to guarantee the prices of certain items like books, but this only delayed the inevitable. Eventually, these other countries fell to the same overwhelming forces.

At some point in the late 2020s, virtually all items were purchased through the One/Net. The products available were often superior and far easier to find. They were delivered to your door, returns were accepted no questions asked and best of all, they were cheaper.

Soon, premium services were made available. The online shops now learned your preferences, your tastes, and did the shopping for you. They not only chose the items you had previously purchased, but selected new ones that their algorithm concluded you would appreciate. Again, if you didn't like something, you could return it at no cost.

If you wanted to alter your pattern of shopping, simply because you were bored or were eager to try something new, that was easy, too. At the click of a changeup button, an entire new repertoire of food, clothes or other items was delivered to you.

Another option was to purchase items that one of your friends had already bought. Again, all you had to do was to go to Friends, scroll to that person's shopping list and, abracadabra, you were shopping like Pablo. Or Antoinette. Or Mary-Sue.

Or better still, and again at a small charge, you could acquire the shopping list of some celebrity or other. Now you could eat like Baba Drago. Dress like Katie Kenny. Or listen to tunes that Niall Smith had danced to that very day in the shower. They made it all so easy.

There was an exception to all this. For those rich enough, special shopping experiences were created. These were model villages, built with small, narrow cobbled streets and charming boutique shops. A boulangerie where the baker stayed up all night preparing the very finest of pastries and tasty treats. A milliner who would help you chose from a wide selection of handmade hats of every shape and size. A florist with the most exotic of flower arrangements. A store where you could purchase hand-crafted soaps and shampoos. Another that made bespoke jewelry according to your individual taste and designs. Such destination shopping experiences were available only, of course, to the super rich. The rest of us purchased our goods on the One/Net.

My Thoughts

These sports that Gran Nancy mentioned sound so interesting. So I looked up "twentieth century sports" on my All-in-One and found a few I've never heard of before. Golf is apparently a game that was played with metal sticks and a small white ball. It ended after water and chemicals could no longer be used to create artificial lawns. The only exception was in places like Scotland where the links grew naturally.

Car racing was another. The races had such peculiar names: Formula 1, 24 Hours of Le Mans, Daytona 500, Indy 500. Apparently these drivers went around and around in circles for hours on end. It sounds pointless!

And then, how about this one: wrapping up in super warm clothing, climbing onto a snowmobile, driving out to a frozen lake, making a hole in the ice, dropping a line to catch a fish, and then retiring to a heated hut and waiting. That doesn't even sound like a sport!

I looked up the word surrogacy in Gran's dictionary. All I could find is "a person in authority appointed to act in place of another." It did not have anything about giving birth. What happens when a dictionary becomes out of date? Will this history, Gran's history, also become out of date? And if so, when?

Also, "time of the month"? Why can't Gran Nancy just say period or menstruation? What is it with old people and not being able to talk about the thing that happens to half the people on the planet? I'm fourteen and I can talk about this, why can't my gran?

I heard back from the school alumni association. They have no contact for Paula, but they do for Midge and Benji. I sent them both a message. Midge replied immediately.

"Quentin made us laugh. Had fire in belly, always angry, always telling us about some injustice or other. A terrible rugby player."

All Benji wrote was: "meet @ gd juice bar. 63rd flr. 6pm Tues. I'm tall."

2029

When I was young, one of my great moments of pride was casting a ballot for the first time. It was in the sixties, and we were determined to make things better. I felt, my friends felt, that our parents were old and out of touch. They didn't understand our generation or the issues that we faced.

In America, they had the civil rights movement. In France, England and other countries, it was all about peace, women's empowerment, and rock and roll. In Germany, the younger generation was challenging their parents and grandparents about what they did during the Nazi period.

It may be hard for you to imagine, but when I was just starting out, women were not paid the same as men at work. Banks would not give us loans without the permission of our husbands or fathers. On the other hand, and just as bad, men had almost no rights over their own children.

I was born in 1948, just a few years after the end of the Second World War and just twenty years since all adult women in Britain were given — or I should say won — the right to vote. When it came my turn to cast a ballot, I took my responsibility very seriously. I studied the policies of each candidate and took a judgment as to who would make the most difference. Usually, I was disappointed. But this did not stop me from doing the same at the next election, and the next.

When it was my children's turn to vote, I saw the same passion. The same hope. The same seriousness. The same belief in the power of the ballot box. Sometimes their "side" won, and they were delighted. Often they were disappointed, but they believed in the system and were committed to upholding it.

Even as far back as the start of the One/Net in the 1990s, people were talking about voting online. Once the technical difficulties were overcome — which was relatively easy — the challenge became a matter of security. In a modern democracy, if power and authority came from voting, and if voting took place online, then how best to protect the process from sabotage and hijacking?

In the mid 2020s, and after several successful trials in various towns and cities across Europe, the technology was tried out for a full national election. To general delight, the government that introduced the new system delivered the project on time and under budget.

Once the voting took place, everything looked positive. The results were produced quicker and with more certainty, allowing for a stable transition of power. And the electorate looked favorably upon the ruling government that had implemented the new voting system with efficiency and prudence.

The problems came a week later, when it became clear that a quarter of the ballots were fake. These phantom voters were either dead or entirely made up. The system had been hacked by a foreign power who preferred one candidate over the other. Worst of all, the file of how people voted was leaked online. This was an absolute violation of the principle of a secret ballot.

After the sabotage was revealed, the country descended into chaos. The losing candidate contested the vote, and it was only after a vicious fight in the highest court that a new election was called. This time by paper ballot. The experiment was such a disaster that no other country dared to organize online voting. Until autumn 2029. That was the moment of the World Parliament election.

It is hard to imagine a time before the WP, but as you know, it is the planet's first global governing body. Up till then we had various international organizations, each with its own acronym, making for a confusing alphabet soup of names: United Nations (UN), World Trade Organization (WTO), International Panel on Climate Change (IPCC), European and North American Security Organization (ENASO), and so on. But the delegates to all these organizations were appointed by national governments. None of these were directly elected by the people.

The idea of a global paper ballot was too much for even the most ambitious of election officers. With more than 10 billion people living on Earth, of which 75 percent were eligible to vote, the only way to organize the election was digitally. By this point, 98.5 percent of the planet had access to the One/Net, so online voting seemed a viable option.

This meant that the security for online voting had to be solved. It took a sophisticated approach. A three-step authentication was used to ensure that only eligible voters could cast their ballot. End-to-end-to-end encryption (E3) was deployed to protect the secret ballot and to ensure votes were not tampered with. And to give people confidence, receipts were given, allowing voters to check their vote had been counted on a public bulletin board.

The days after the election were marked not by scandal of vote tampering or stories of foreign interference, but instead by the normal celebrations of the winning parties followed by a discussion about how the victors would form the first World Parliament.

From this point forward, paper ballots were discarded into the rubbish bin of history.

Notebook 7

My Thoughts

I have decided not to get upset by Gran Nancy's way of telling history. It's a little rambly and too much about our family — not really world events — but I promised to write down Gran's words verbatim. Which is what I'm doing.

This whole paper voting thing seems a little idiotic to me. I mean, how hard can it be to organize a digital election? I'm sure there were technical difficulties, but really! I am finding it hard not to judge my ancestors. Sorry, everyone. xoxoxo

As instructed, I went to the Good Smoothie Bar on the sixty-third floor. Standing outside was a very tall, very thin person, probably seventy-something, wearing a blue jacket, blue trousers and blue boots. According to Gran, Quentin was born in 1974, so any classmates must be about the same age. It had to be Benji.

The typical person waiting outside a bar would be glued to their All-in-One. Watching a show, catching up on the news or communicating with a friend. Instead, Benji was eyes up, searching left and right, as if checking to see if anyone was following. Alert. Nervous. On guard.

Stranger still, Benji was occupied with flipping a web of string in his hands this way and that, almost unconsciously, never looking down at the newly formed configurations. It was all a little unsettling, but I pushed myself to overcome my anxiety and introduced myself.

"Hi there," I said, "I'm Billy."

"I'm Benji. I use they/them pronouns. What are yours?"

I was confused! "Just call me Billy," I said.

Then I felt uncomfortable. What if Benji thought I was judging?

"You look like Quentin," Benji said with a smile. Which made me feel a little better.

So I asked, "What's with all the string?"

"It's a cat's cradle," Benji replied, sounding a little frustrated. "My Navajo grandparent showed me this one pattern called Two Coyotes Running Apart. I've spent the past month trying to remember how to do it but I can't get it right."

We went inside and ordered drinks. We then had an awkward moment almost immediately. When the juice-maker asked, "Would your friend like ice?" I said, "I don't know, I will have to ask … them."

I hope Benji wasn't offended by the pause. Normally I would just use a person's name, or their situation or description, like teacher, waiter, or in Benji's case, friend.

But as it was important to Benji, I would of course use "they" and "them."

When we were sitting at a table, I tried talking about

Quentin but Benji just changed the subject. They kept tapping their fingers on their knee. Their eyes were wild, and they spoke too fast. They kept looking over their shoulder like someone was watching them.

After less than five minutes Benji said it was time to go. And then I was by myself with my pomelo, carrot and ginger juice. Was all very strange.

Later, I looked up cat's cradle in Gran's dictionary. It said that it was a game for children in which players produce symmetrical figures. The first record of it in literature was in 1768. The All-in-One gave more information. Apparently, the game is played around the world. The Native Hawaiians call it "hei" or "net." In Indonesia, they call it "toeka-toeka," or "ladder-ladder." In China, "well rope." I wonder what Two Coyotes Running Apart looks like?

Must remember to ask Gran Nancy about they and them. My gran is the only person I know who says she and he when talking about people. Maybe Gran knows about using they and them, too?

2031

In the 2010s, many of my friends started using the pronouns "they" and "them." They said that they did not want to identify as either male or female, describing themselves as nonbinary. They said that using the words "his" or "her" was problematic

I understood their concerns. Language is powerful. It can make a big difference. In all languages, there are certain words that are considered hateful. And language reflects the values of the society of that time. Which words are used. Which words are not used. Even into the 2020s, it was still possible to read newspaper articles that used "mankind" instead of "humankind," or "headmaster" rather than "school principal." That described domestic chores as "women's work," or used expressions like "man up" or "fights like a girl."

As a woman, this upset me every time. Each language — German, English, Mandarin, Spanish, French — had its own problems. There was a huge need to open things up, to make books, articles, TV shows and speeches more inclusive. To adapt to the changing values of society. Which I totally supported.

So some people wanted to identify as neither male or female, and most people were fine with that. We soon started seeing TV with characters who used they and them.

But more recently, I have noticed fewer people using pronouns at all. Instead, they have found ways of not using he or she or they. The most common solution is to use people's first names. Which is nice, I think, as it is personal. Somehow warmer. That's why you call me Gran Nancy rather than Grandmother or Grandma. The exception to this shift has been certain activists who are committed to the old ways, like Benji. They still like to be called they and them.

I hope that answers your question about language. Now I would like to go back to something else you asked me: What was it like to live through the SHOCK?

In a word, it was terrifying.

For decades, scientists had predicted that if we didn't make dramatic changes in the way we lived, average global temperatures would rise by four degrees by the year 2100. What they got wrong was the timing. The temperature spike occurred in 2030, seventy years earlier than forecast. Which is why they called it the SHOCK.

There were many theories for what happened. The most persuasive was that multiple tipping points happened at the same time, compounding each other — melting of the icecaps, sea-level temperature rise, change in ocean currents. But really the reasons didn't matter. The damage had been done. The disaster that for decades we had spoken of as "in the future," had suddenly arrived.

In parts of the Arctic, the temperature was now more than eight degrees higher than normal. Vast swathes of the planet's ice had already melted. As had the great glaciers of Greenland, Iceland and the Andes. Sea levels were rising fast, made worse by storm surges and higher than usual rainfalls.

Governments tried to delay the inevitable. They built massive dykes and sea walls and deployed vast networks of giant pumps and other anti-flood devices. None of this could stop the fast-rising tide.

The first countries to be hit were the ones who could least afford it. In early 2031, the tiny Pacific islands of Vanuatu and Kiribati were totally submerged. For some time, the sea level had been rising, but many residents hung on until a large storm delivered the coup de grâce. It was awful to read about. I felt so terrible for these poor people. Their lives totally destroyed. They couldn't take anything more than a small bag with them when they were evacuated.

Then the SHOCK spread around the world.

In the months after Vanuatu and Kiribati were submerged, large sections of the world's major coastal cities had to be evacuated: 17 million people from Shanghai, 5 million each in Osaka and Ho Chi Minh City, 3 million people each in Miami, Mumbai and Alexandria, a million each in Rio de Janeiro, Amsterdam and London. We were lucky that we lived on one of London's highest hills. Many of our friends were not so fortunate and had to move to temporary accommodation.

In an attempt to prevent looting, martial law was imposed along all coast lines. Anyone caught in the cities after evacuation orders was put in jail. At an emergency meeting of the World Parliament, the world leaders agreed to an immediate end to all fossil fuels. Though the cost to the economy was enormous — the alternative means of transport, heating and industrial production were not yet fully in place — indecision was now considered impossible.

A shockwave rocked the global economy. Though long predicted, such a dramatic shift to the very fabric of our societies still came to many as a surprise. However, the financial markets responded positively, for the putrid boil of denial and procrastination had been lanced. At last, the world had turned a corner. Though a four-degree rise in temperature was appalling and was having a terrible impact on people and animals around the planet, finally there was hope that the impact of climate change would not get worse. It might even, with a little luck, human ingenuity and patience, be improved.

My Thoughts

I asked why, if the SHOCK was so obvious, Gran Nancy didn't do something about it? Gran scowled. And stormed off. I really think I caused upset. Which I didn't want to do. I love Gran Nancy.

Just as I was wondering what next, Gran came back, some letters in hand. And gave them to me. Most were between Gran Nancy (Professor Nancy Schmidt) and the head of the college (Master Humphries).

There was also a stack of postcards from someone called Rosemary, presumably a friend. They were all old pictures of Venice, a place I'd never heard of. I looked it up on my All-in-One and it said that Venice had been permanently submerged during the sea-level rise of the mid-2020s. There are a lot of postcards from different dates. I will add them in to this notebook at the appropriate year.

Reading the letters and postcards, I was a little surprised. My small little gran, who struggles to get out of a chair without help, who falls asleep during mealtimes, who pinches my cheek and sometimes farts on the way to the bathroom, was a fighter. Not quite sure how to deal with this. There is this person in front of me, 102 years old, amazing for sure, but the most heroic thing my gran does each day is to survive it. And then there is this other person, Gran Nancy but younger, who stood up against those in power and said, "We have to do something." And was right, even though nobody listened. Again. And again. And again. Year after year.

I looked up the word "their" in Gran Nancy's dictionary. It said it was the plural for he or she. But it also said that it was sometimes used instead of him or her, "when the gender is uncertain or inconclusive." That was back in 1971! Perhaps Benji wasn't so radical after all.

Katia came over. We did some schoolwork together. It was nice to just focus on normal stuff. Before leaving, Katia said goodbye to Gran Nancy. So thoughtful.

I also saw Benji again. I was writing up my latest conversation with Gran Nancy when they walked in.

"What's that?" Benji asked, their focus half on me and half on manipulating the string between their hands. Apparently, they still have not solved Two Coyotes Running Apart.

So I explained about my interview project. Something seemed to happen, like a thought train was triggered.

"Can I read it?" they said.

By now I was on to my seventh notebook, so I handed over the second one, the one with the *Guardian* article, but made them promise to keep it safe. I thought, maybe if Benji saw what I was doing, they might tell me about

Quentin. Now I am not sure. What happens if the notebook gets lost and all that work is wasted?

Worried that this history is becoming too personal. I will ask Gran Nancy to tell me about events that effected everyone.

From: Daniel Humphries <DH242@cam.ac.uk>
Subject: Your manuscript
Date: June 1, 2028 at 8:22:49 PM GMT+1
To: Nancy Schmidt <NS998@cam.ac.uk >

Dear Professor Schmidt,

I have looked at your manuscript as requested and, as you asked for my feedback, I will provide it. I hope I will not cause undue offense.

I have one major comment. Since you are a professor of sixteenth-century history, Elizabeth I and her court, why did you write about the current climate crisis?

Surely the role of the historian is to be objective, not to focus on a subject simply because it excites her personally.

Yours truly,

Master Humphries

From: Nancy Schmidt <NS998@cam.ac.uk>
Subject: re: Your manuscript
Date: June 4, 2028 at 5:07:26 PM GMT+1
To: Master Humphries <DH242@cam.ac.uk>

Dear Master Humphries,

Thank you for taking the time to read my efforts.

It is obvious to me that our species is facing a truly life-threatening situation. So while researching the court of Queen Elizabeth I is endlessly fascinating, it bears little on today's crisis.

My interest is to produce a work that can make a difference. If this means changing my focus of study to contemporary politics, then that is what I will do.

Yours fondly,

Nancy

From: Nancy Schmidt <NS998@cam.ac.uk>
Subject: re: Your manuscript
Date: November 3, 2029 at 4:35:03 PM GMT
To: Master Humphries <DH242@cam.ac.uk>

Dear Master Humphries,

We really must organize the faculty to put pressure on
the government to take action about climate change.
If we do not make dramatic and immediate changes to
our way of life we will be in big trouble. When our children look back at what we did, they will ask which side
of history we were on. How will you answer them?

Yours sincerely,

Nancy Schmidt

From: Daniel Humphries <DH242@cam.ac.uk>
Subject: re: Your manuscript
Date: 5 January, 2030 at 3:35:55 AM GMT
To: Nancy Schmidt <NS998@cam.ac.uk>

Dear Professor Schmidt,

Thank you for all your letters but I really must ask you to stop writing to me. The College is aware of your concerns, but as you know, we are an academic institution. It is not our job to meddle in politics.

And could you please cease your protests outside the college each evening? Besides the fact that your students should instead be in their rooms working, there are now so many gathered that it is proving difficult for others to enter the college. Again, I remind you of your responsibility as a member of the history faculty and the higher purpose of learning.

Yours sincerely,

Master Humphries

Nancy,   3.4.31

I cannot write much as I have to leave now with my family. The city is flooded and we must find higher ground. Watching the Shock unfold over the last two years I see that you were right all along. I do hope you will forgive me.

Your friend,
Rosemary xx

2032

I remember the moment as if it was yesterday ...

The year was 1969 — I was at home with your gran Jack. We had just started dating. We were sitting in the living room with my parents gathered around the television — an electronic box that showed programs beamed over the airwaves. After quite a long wait the announcer said the moment had finally arrived. And then it happened. Neil Armstrong the American astronaut climbed down the ladder and stepped onto the Moon.

When I watched Armstrong bounce along the surface of the Moon I could not stop crying. I found it overwhelming, that we, humans, had the technical and organizational ability to mount a space mission. Remarkable.

And then, sixty-three years later, there was the next giant step for humankind. We were about to establish a permanent settlement on the Moon.

I give credit to our entire species, for without the contributions of tens of thousands of people, from a multitude of countries, taking decades and decades of extraordinary effort, diligence and creativity, this singular accomplishment would not have been possible.

It was a coincidence, of course, that the inauguration of MoonBase1 took place just months after the WP finally intervened in the climate SHOCK, for the preparations had taken years. But such timing made this occasion even more poignant. It came at the exact point that billions of women and men around the world were asking themselves a profound and deeply troubling question: Can our planet sustain long-term habitat for the human species? The obvious next question was, if not the Earth, then where?

The answer was space.

Or to be more exact, our solar system. To Mars and then perhaps later the planets beyond. And to get to these, it was agreed that a launch site had to be built on the Moon. To send spaceships to and from the Earth required too much energy. It was much more efficient to organize our space voyages from the Moon.

I remember these few minutes clearly. I was at the city cinema along with tens of thousands of others. We watched the action live upon the enormous screen. The first lunar module landed softly upon the Moon's surface. Then another, and then another. There were hundreds of them. It reminded me of British and American soldiers parachuting down into France in those old Second World War movies. The modules were seventy times the size of the craft that Armstrong and his team used all those years before. Really, they should have been called space buses. For their task was to transport humans from Earth to the Moon, over and over again.

I watched in awe as the hatches opened, and they all came out. The technicians and engineers and administrators. The botanists and extra-terrestrial urban designers. Hundreds of them. Each carrying a bag of personal items. They would be preparing the ground, readying the "homes" for the new arrivals. This felt like the moment of actual colonization.

The camera crew followed the space voyagers along a wide path lined with blinking lights toward what looked like a small hill. I was struck by how bleak the landscape looked. Rocks, dust, sinkholes. I am sure it was extremely exciting for the pioneers. Life changing. But in truth I would not have liked to have been there. At least not yet. Until they made things a little more comfortable. A little more, dare I say, human. I felt sorry for them.

As they neared the rocky outcrop, it was possible to see an opening. The group entered, and, after taking a lift down twenty stories and traveling through a series of airlocks and sanitizers, they removed their protective clothing. They were now inside the bio-chamber.

They would stay on the Moon for the next five years. This in itself was a huge achievement. Until this point, the longest contiguous amount of time a human had ever spent in space was 437 days. This was by the Russian cosmonaut Valeri Polyakov in 1994 aboard the Mir space station. The reason for the time limit in space was because human bodies had evolved to function in Earth's gravity and, over the years, scientists had learned that astronauts experienced severe physical problems in the gravity-free environment of space. Their muscles atrophied. Their hearts shrank. Their bone tissue was absorbed, causing kidney stones and fractures.

The good news was that the Moon's gravity was five-sixths that of Earth, so these problems would, it was hoped, be far less. Part of the mission of MoonBase1 was to see if long-term extra-terrestrial habitation was not only possible but healthy.

A weak gravity was just the start of the problems. Besides the logistical nightmare of transporting all the food and water the settlers would need whilst on the Moon, another serious threat was the Moon's insubstantial atmosphere, which allowed for extreme temperature fluctuations. The thin atmosphere also failed to protect the surface from cosmic rays such as solar flares — whose radiation was dangerous to humans. The solution was for the humans to live deep underground, their bio-dome constructed inside one of the many huge caves found under the Moon's crust. Work and travel on the surface would be severely restricted.

Another key challenge was the provision of energy. Given that the lunar night was 354 hours (or 14.75 Earth days), solar farms had been built across the Moon's surface to ensure continuous supply. Travel to and maintenance of these power plants would be difficult but essential. Another critical task would be the construction of additional bio-domes to allow for the influx of hundreds and then thousands more colonists.

There would be many more news feeds to watch, but

for now this was enough. The live stream came to an end with a close-up of the new arrivals smiling and waving from MoonBase1. I joined the tens of thousands around me who were loudly applauding. I noticed that I was not the only person wiping away tears of pride as I walked back to my little apartment that evening.

Since then, I have heard some people question the value of this remarkable space mission. Was it worth the vast expense? they ask. What benefit does it bring us? The snarkier ones said that MoonBase1 was just a hobby for one of the wealthy Ethnarchs. I can't remember which one. Perhaps the woman who runs that social media platform you young people are always using. To me, though, it was more than that. It was the first and most important step for us to build a long-term alternative to Planet Earth. It was our insurance policy.

My Thoughts

Would I want to leave Earth? It would be amazing to see our home planet from space. And I would love to know what it feels like to walk around in lower gravity. But I don't think I would want to live in a cave on the Moon. Even for a year. Even if it was super high tech and had lots of cool features. I would want to breathe normal air. Makes me appreciate my family, the life I have.

Benji is blanking me. I've sent at least five messages and no response. Asked Midge for help. Midge said, "That sounds like Benji." Totally unhelpful. What is wrong with these people? I'm freaking out. Not sure what to do.

Gran Nancy has come down with something. The doctor says it's an infection. This is a real worry. Now that so many bacteria have become drug resistant, the use of antibiotics is severely restricted. Children and young adults are the priority, not old people like Gran Nancy who, and, I hate to say this, does look old. Like the end is near.

Katia was going to come over, but I said that Gran Nancy wasn't feeling well. A few minutes later a voice note arrived on my All-in-One. It was Katia singing a song for

Gran Nancy (how sweet is that!), promising to stop by after school later in the week. I'm lucky to have Katia as a friend.

When Gran Nancy feels a little better — and I hope that will be soon — I will try and move the conversation along quicker. We aren't even halfway through the history yet. I haven't even been born! We need to spin through the years faster or we might not get to the more recent times.

Notebook 9

2034

Patience, Billy, patience.

There's one more thing I want to mention before we get to the year you were born.

It happened in 2033. Looking back from today, the delay seems so surprising. The resistance to change must have been immense. From the farmers, the shopkeepers, the restaurant owners and of course most of all, the consumers.

The date will go down in human history as one of the most important. Like August 1, 1834, when slavery was abolished in the British Empire. Or November 28, 1893, when women first voted in New Zealand. Or May 8, 1945, when the idea of racial supremacy was defeated in Germany. Or April 29, 1997, when the use of chemical weapons in warfare was outlawed across the globe.

And what was this momentous date? It was as simple as it was profound. For, on September 26, 2033, it became illegal worldwide to eat meat.

The consumption of animal products had been decreasing for years. Some people were vegetarian on health grounds. The eating of red meat, for instance, was a cause of high cholesterol. Others felt that the raising of cattle consumed too many resources. That our planet could not afford the luxury of everyone eating meat. Still more argued that the killing of animals was immoral, saying that cows, fish, pigs and chickens are all sentient beings and therefore have a right to live a long and healthy life.

And from this, it was only a short step to argue that humans had no right to steal animal products such as milk, eggs or honey. Long gone are the days when a metal sucking machine was strapped to the udder of a lactating cow, their milk then drunk by human children.

It was still possible to find bags, gloves, coats, shoes and belts made of animal skin, but only in the most expensive of vintage shops. It had been more than ten years since medicines had been tested on animals. Meanwhile, plant-based "meat" was available that not only tasted and looked as good as meat but was far cheaper.

At the start of 2033, less than 15 percent of the world's population consumed and used any form of animal product. I have to confess that we were part of the 15 percent. Our family had always loved meat. Barbecue ribs. Roast beef. A homemade hamburger. Steak and kidney pie. Herb sausages. Coq au vin. All delicious. Even thinking of these dishes makes me drool.

Jack's gran was a butcher from the east end of London. As were his parents and grandparents before that. The special skills required to kill an animal cleanly were passed down through the generations like a secret sauce. It was in the blood, so to speak. And while we understood all the arguments against the eating of meat, we felt that if the animals were reared carefully, so that they could enjoy their lives to the full, then it was fine.

To us, consuming beef, pork and poultry was organic, pure and natural. After all, why were we born with canine teeth if not for eating meat? And wasn't eating vegetables AND meat what made us omnivores, one of our key human traits that went back all the way to the time that hominids roamed the wide savanna grasslands of Africa? Everything in moderation, we told ourselves.

So we ate meat, but much less than in the old days. Once a month on average, never more than once a week.

But Quentin had stopped eating meat long ago. I do remember a conversation years before the ban.

We were at the dinner table and your auncle Quentin asked me, "How can you eat meat when you don't need to? It's so cruel." I looked at him and I realized that I didn't have a good answer.

By the end of 2033, everything had changed. It had been long known that animals felt pain, and to overcome this, butchers such as Jack's family had made their killing "humane," using techniques that allowed for quick and clean deaths.

But now, following dramatic improvements in inter-species communication at universities in Europe and Asia, humans began hearing directly from the animals themselves. It appeared that animals experienced fear or anxiety before they were butchered.

In one epoch-changing exchange, a pig transmitted the following words: *NO KILL*. This was too much for even the most die-hard meat eaters. The final decision was made by the WP when it became clear that animals felt the trauma of the meat trade. And so, meat was made illegal.

Within a few years, as if by magic, the decision became obvious to everyone. Just as it had after the abolition of slavery or after every adult was given the right to vote, it became incomprehensible to consume animal products: their flesh, eggs, skin, bone or tusks. To eat an animal has become as wrong as eating another human being. It's not only illegal, it has become taboo.

One of the consequences of this meat ban was the near total disappearance of domesticated animals from the countryside. In the US alone, it took only five years for the number of cattle to collapse from almost 100 million to less than 100,000. Those that were kept were held for scientific use and zoos.

In New Zealand, where there had been almost 40 million sheep, or nearly 10 sheep for every person in the country, there were now fewer than 10,000. But the biggest obliteration of all was for chickens. Within twenty-four months of the meat ban, the number of chickens fell from 20 billion to less than 1 million. In China alone, they saw the loss of more than 5 billion chickens.

Of all the animal-protection laws, the one I found hardest to accept was the Horse Act. For centuries, humans and horses had worked in harmony together. Plowing the fields of Northern Europe, rounding up the cattle in the American West, trekking across the Mongolian Steppes. I understood the argument that some riders treated their animals cruelly, overusing the bit and the whip. But to outlaw human-horse collaboration seemed a step too far. Maybe even two steps too far.

I remember walking in the countryside a few years after the ban and being overwhelmed by the change. There were no sheep bleating in the fields. No horses neighing in the paddocks. No cattle walking around looking for the next patch to chew. Where it was impossible to grow crops, birds and other wildlife had returned. It felt so strange. But like all things, we quickly got used to it.

Of course, there were wild animals. In the US, there were black bears, gray wolves, pumas and elk. In Europe, we had mountain goats, badgers, reindeer and wild boar. In parts of Africa, elephants, lions, giraffes and zebras. But for the most part, they kept away from human settlements.

There *was* a rise in the sea's animal population. For fishing was also banned, and before long, marine biologists noticed an increase in aquatic life.

Farm animals were not the only ones to be impacted. Given the food and energy shortages that came after the SHOCK, it was considered both impractical and immoral to own a pet. The laws regarding custody were ambiguous, but the strong suggestion was that you give up your pets.

Many found it incredibly hard to part with their dogs or cats or tortoises. In fact, of all the changes I have seen over the past decades, this was perhaps the one that people struggled with the most. The pets were taken away to farms in the countryside where they were neutered and spent their last years until they died naturally. A few people kept their pets, taking care of them in secret. Feeding them on scraps behind closed doors. But this was sadly the exception, not the rule.

Within a shockingly short period, human interaction with non-human animals came to an abrupt halt. After centuries of intense mutual dependency, the planet was separated between the human and the non-human worlds.

My Thoughts

I went to Gran Nancy's bedpod. It was time to keep going
with the history. I was so happy to see Gran feeling better:
redder cheeks, sparkly eyes, teasing me a little. But there
was something else, something different. I think Gran
realizes that time might be running out. Like the seconds
have become more precious, urgent.

We spoke for a few minutes, then it became clear that
Gran Nancy needed a rest. Before I left, my gran gave
me the invitation to Auncle Quentin's funeral service. I
wasn't sure what to say or what to do. I hugged Gran. That
seemed to make things better. I hope we speak about this
some more but don't want to add pressure. I wish I had
met Quentin.

Thinking back on my conversation with my gran, it
does sound nice to have a pet in the house. I wonder what
it was like to have a purring cat asleep in your bedpod or
to throw a stick for a dog? Come here, Fido, here! It must
have been fun.

Got a message from Benji. Finally! They weren't blanking me. They were in custody. Wouldn't tell me more

by One/Net. Wants to meet in person. Will try and get together in the next few days.

We are almost at the time I come into the story. I'm excited to see what happens. I hope that I will remember some of the events. That will make things interesting. I can check Gran Nancy's memory against mine.

In small proportions we just beauties see;
And in short measures life may perfect be.
Ben Jonson

CELEBRATING THE LIFE OF
Quentin Henry Schmidt

IN LO...

Quentin Henry Schmidt

June 29, 1974 – October 15, 2033

"But I could have told you,
This world was never meant
For one as Beautiful as you."
"VINCENT", DON MCLEAN

...LL BEARERS

Robert Johnson   David Hirst
Benjamin Rothenbaum   Yasmeen Akhtar
Petra Florentina   Theodore Best

FUNERAL SERVICE
Tuesday, October 30, 2033, 10.00am
Granchester Meadow (near Red Lion),
Cambridgeshire, England

ORDER OF SERVICE
Welcome
It's The End of the World as We Know it (REM)
Remembrance (Benji)
Poem (Professor Nancy Schmidt)
I need to Wake Up (Etheridge)

PRIEST
Tulip Azizi

ACKNOWLEDGEMENT
We are sincerely grateful to the many friends who have
given us support and comfort during this time of loss.
Your presence helped to lighten our burden.

My dearest Nancy

21.10.33

I was totally shocked when I heard the news about
Quentin. I am so sorry I could not make the funeral.
Shall I come see you? With much fondest love.

Rosemary

Nancy

4.1.34

I do hope you have received my cards. I have not heard from you. I try and imagine what it must be like for you, but of course I have no idea. Please do not feel any obligation to write to me but know this, you are truly loved.

Truly, truly loved.
R.

2035

This was the year of the hospital miracle!

I am so thankful. To Tim Berners-Lee, to Vince Cerf, to Peter Kirstein — the founders of the One/Net all those years ago.

Why am I so thankful? Because in 2035 your life was saved because of them.

Your mother was much younger than your father — she was forty-four — and you were so small when you came out. A few months later, your throat and tongue swelled up, you started vomiting violently, you struggled to breathe. I was terrified. Especially after we had just lost Quentin.

When we rushed you to the hospital they checked all available medical data about our family via the One/Net and, because all medical records had been digitized and shared amongst every medical establishment, they then realized that Gran Jack had a bad allergy to oats, and the oat milk that was being fed to you in addition to your mother's milk had caused a reaction in you. This data saved your life.

Ever since the start of digital records, hospitals have

been obsessed, rightly in my opinion, with privacy. Because the technology did not exist to protect people's data, each hospital or medical group had their own data system, which meant sharing information was impossible. But since the arrival of FDP, or Full Data Protection as it is properly known, data can only be unlocked by the data's owner, or a power of attorney. So critical information, such as health records, can be safely stored and accessed only by those who have a legitimate reason to want to do so.

Of course, this breakthrough only happened after the Net Wars.

The First Net War took place between China and the US. For years, China had placed restrictions on the One/Net, preventing its population from using Google (then the largest company on Earth, before a journalist uncovered the big scandal) and other search engines.

To puncture this so-called Great Firewall of China, the president of the US launched an economic blockade, prompting immediate economic retaliation from China and its allies. Soon the two countries were locked in a death spiral that crashed the world stock markets and threatened a major economic recession. When the streets of Hong Kong, Shanghai and Beijing filled with millions of protestors, the Chinese government realized they had no choice and took down the Firewall. For the first time, digital material was available to anyone with One/Net access around the world.

Then came the Second Net War. This was triggered by

the world's largest digital provider announcing that they were splitting the One/Net into three different strata.

Saturn would be most expensive, with the highest speeds and the best content. Neptune offered decent programs and data, but was considerably slower than Saturn. And Pluto, which was free, contained barely any interesting content — mostly government announcements, weather, religious broadcasts and financial reports — and was only accessible at agonizingly slow speeds.

Within days, billions of people and millions of companies were effectively cut off from the One/Net. By now, access to digital information had become as essential as the air we breathe or the food we eat. It was a question both of national and personal security. The One/Net of things was everywhere and foundational to our lives. It impacted the rate at which a pacemaker beat in a person's heart; the orientation of a hundred thousand wind turbines that powered a billion homes; the altitude, velocity and angle of travel of more than five hundred weather satellites.

People were adjusting to this new system when disaster struck. In 2033, we were hit by a massive solar flare that took out a large section of the One/Net. The light was so bright that people were woken up thinking it was morning. Many were struck by the light's beauty, with rich purples, blues and greens swirling through the skies. The last time the planet was struck like this was back in 1859, the Carrington Event, which caused a massive blackout in the world's telegraph system. The solar flare of 2033 was one crisis too many for the Ethnarchs. They simply couldn't have the One/Net so vulnerable to failure.

The solution was radical. The World Parliament globalized the One/Net and invested huge amounts of money to safeguard us from future solar flares. From this moment forward, it was considered a planetary asset, like the oceans or atmosphere, and was to be made available to all humans on a free and open basis.

One of the benefits of this bold step, was that the policing of the One/Net could be centralized. For years, we had suffered the horrors of One/Net abuse. People had written ugly, upsetting, terrible things about other people on social media sites. But little could be done about these digital vandals. In the US and Europe they were called trolls; in Japan "arashi," which meant "laying waste"; in Thailand "krian," or "boy with close-cropped haircut"; and in China "white eye," meaning without iris or pupil. These scourges created fake accounts and hid behind false IP addresses located in countries that provided no data protection or accountability.

Now that the One/Net was owned by the WP, action was not only possible, it was swift. Within three months a database of trolls was created — known as the Villains of the One/Net — and online abuse fell from the tens of millions to the hundreds. You heard that right, hundreds. For one simple reason. If a troll was caught, and the person behind the abuse traced to an individual — which was now possible — they were banned from the One/Net for life. This was such a heinous punishment that it deterred almost every troll, krian and white eye on the planet.

Following the globalization of the One/Net, dramatic progress was made on data security. This led to FDP. Which is what saved your life.

Nancy,

That was so lovely! I so enjoyed spending a week with you. Oh, the pastries! Those fresh strawberries! They reminded me of the ones we used to have in Venice. How I miss that beautiful city. And it was so fabulous to meet your new granddaughter. What a beautiful baby Billy is! Do write soon.

Love
Rosemary

5.7.35

My Thoughts

After I turned off my All-in-One, I told Gran Nancy that I felt a little weird to see my name mentioned by Rosemary and am now wondering if I should include myself in this history. Instead of answering the question directly, Gran Nancy told me a story.

There is a beautiful clock built into a white stone tower overlooking a square in the city of Padua, Italy, my gran said. It is perhaps the oldest clock in the world, made in 1344. It is a twenty-four–hour clock, so the hand that is adorned with a sun symbol goes around once a day, not twice as is normal. Around the outside of the clock are the signs of the Zodiac. And at the center sits the Earth, because back in 1344 people thought the Sun went around the Earth.

The point is, Gran Nancy continued, the people hundreds of years ago understood that the Sun and the planets were circulating around the Earth. But they got the perspective wrong.

The question is not whether you are in the history I am sharing, Gran said. The question is what is your position in that history?

Benji came to see me and gave me the missing notebook. I was cross that it had taken so long, but I was happy to have it back, so I was friendly.

Benji said, "I wish more people had listened to what we were trying to say about climate change. They knew the SHOCK would happen, but they did nothing about it."

These were exactly my thoughts, so I replied, "I wish we could tell them." Then Benji stopped all their pacing and jiggling. I had never seen them so still before. Unmoving. They didn't even blink.

"What if we could?" they said. This made no sense to me.

"What if we could what?" I asked.

"What if we could send a message back?"

I started laughing, but I was the only one. It was clear Benji was serious. They asked for the notebook back.

This set me laughing again. "No way," I said. "You only just returned it."

But they had a steely look in their eye. So I handed it over.

It was then that I noticed that Benji wasn't carrying any string between their fingers, so I asked if they'd made progress on Two Coyotes Running Apart. They looked at me glumly.

"Maybe my gran didn't teach it to me after all," they said. "Perhaps it's a false memory."

Now, writing that last sentence down, I wonder if I misheard what Benji said about "sending a message back." I must have.

Gran Nancy has more energy today. Apparently, Katia came by earlier with some chocolates. "Such a nice friend," Gran said.

I decided it was time to keep going with the history. As Gran Nancy often states, "Make hay while the sun shines." It felt a little too soon to ask more questions about Quentin, so I focused on happier memories. I asked what people did for entertainment, and how did this change over the years?

Notebook 10

2037

Growing up in the 1950s and 1960s, I went to the cinema (I really loved the detective stories) and cheered on my local football team (we won the national cup three times!). I skated on the local pond when it froze over, and my friends and I bought lemonade and sweets at the corner store. These were small pleasures, but they made me happy.

Later when I was a young adult, I'd go with a date to dance parties. Our favorite music was the Beatles, the Temptations and Aretha Franklin. After I married Jack, we would take our children Quentin and Robert to some pretty spot in the park, lay out a blanket and eat home-made food. Cheese sandwiches, potato balls, pholourie with mango chutney and salara. What we called a picnic. How quaint!

I should pause for a moment, and talk about that phrase I just used, "young adult." It is interesting how much the meaning of words has evolved as the years pass. We used to see a lifespan as having only four parts: childhood, adult, middle age and old age. Now of course, given that many of us live to 120 or 130, these labels no longer apply.

We now speak of eight phases:

infancy (0 to 5)
childhood (5 to 20)
juvenile time (20s and 30s)
young adulthood (40s and 50s)
early mid years (60s and 70s)
late mid years (80s and 90s)
mature years (100s and 110s)
elder years (120s and onwards)

Some scientists predicted that, as we lived longer, our appearance would change. We would become younger looking. This is what has happened in the canine family. Compared to their wolf ancestors, dogs now have shortened snouts and wide-set eyes like puppies. They call this process "juvenilization" or "neoteny." The scientists said that humans would soon develop larger heads, flatter faces, and shorter arms and legs. So far, we haven't seen this, which is probably a good thing. But if people keep living longer, maybe it will happen in a few generations.

When we were young, the magic age was eighteen. How I dreamed of being that age as a kid. Once I was eighteen, I told myself, I would be an adult. I would be able to drive a car, graduate from school, drink alcohol and get a job. I would leave home and find my own apartment.

Things have changed so much. These days, hardly anybody leaves their parents' home until their 30s. Many stay well into their 40s. It is just too expensive to rent your own place. In effect, you and my other grandchildren will experience longer childhoods. You will start being responsible for yourself a decade after my children were. Maybe more.

In some ways, I think this is a good thing. Less stress. More opportunity to have fun, to explore your likes and dislikes, to try on different personalities, experiment with life, before settling on the identity you will wear for the rest of your lives. Yet, I also feel a little nostalgic for the reckless adventure of our formative years. The heady excess. The danger. The risk of getting it wrong with consequences, so that it really mattered.

There's been another big change since my childhood. And I find it hard to even say this, but when I was growing up we put our old people into special homes. I know, it sounds so cruel. One day they would be living by themselves, able to make their own food, do their own shopping, take themselves to visit friends, and the next they lost all their independence. They quickly became confused and forgetful. They were lonely and miserable. So the people who ran the homes gave them happy drugs, which made it easier to manage things. But now the old people were a shadow of their former selves. It was all so sad.

Today, of course, it's all different. We know that the more stimulation we have, including those of longer years, the better it is for our health. So, where is the best place for a mature person or elder to live? Why, with their children, grandchildren and great-grandchildren, of course.

The noise and activity is good for them. The love. The attention. The drama. Even your moods, Billy!

And perhaps most importantly, it is good for mature people and elders to be surrounded by people who can remember the old stories, the family jokes. For if we are nothing else, we humans are storytellers. After all, why do you think we dream every night? We are biologically wired to create narratives that include characters, conflict and excitement. Who better to tell stories to than your closest relatives?

Forgive me. I became side-tracked. Let me get back to entertainment.

In my 40s and 50s we had so much fun! Two decades of bliss. It was a golden age of luxury. We worked hard, attended rock concerts, went shopping and had dinner parties with our friends. I purchased expensive presents for my dear Jack. I bought clothes and books and makeup for me. And for our children, toys and games whenever I felt like it.

For my entire life, I'd go to a store and hope they'd have what I was looking for. It was hit and miss. More often than not I would be disappointed and would have to accept whatever they had in stock. But then One/Net shopping became ubiquitous when I was in my 60s, and it became a joy. With a click of a button I could order the weekly groceries and have them delivered to our front door. I could order a hard-to-find part for my car, or a piece of vintage glass, or whatever it was that interested me. It was like a miracle.

And best of all we traveled. Oh, how we traveled. Airplane flights were remarkably cheap. We could go anywhere in the world. It took just five minutes to go onto the One/Net, book a flight to another country and it was all organized. When we arrived, we rented a car and could journey wherever we liked. We stayed in a lovely hotel, so all our needs were taken care of. It was simply divine! There was no limit to where we could go. What we could consume.

But then, as you know, things began to change. The 2020s brought about one crisis and then the next. Finally, the government told us that we had been consuming too many resources. That the planet could not take it anymore. And that we now had to be frugal.

I remember seeing the same catchphrase again and again on posters in the streets, on buses and online. It has stuck in my head even after all these years. It went like this:

IF YOU WANT MORE TOMORROW,
LIVE LESS TODAY.

This meant less shopping. Less travel. Fewer new things. More repairing of old items. More recycling. More making do. And living in more efficient homes.

So, our leisure time changed once again. We still watched movies, and believe me, they were incredible! The storylines were so emotional, thrilling and complex. The visual and sound effects were remarkable. The acting superb.

I call it "acting," but in fact it had been a long time since we stopped watching human actors. It started with children's movies about animals. The studios had developed technology where computers could produce images of lions, elephants, apes and the landscapes in which they lived that were so convincing that they looked real. They called this "photo-realism."

Soon they were applying this to human characters with great success. To make the transition convincing, directors used footage of actors from old movies and built their new characters upon this. People couldn't tell that they were watching computer-generated human actors. Instead, they were amazed at what these movie stars could do. Jump from vehicle to vehicle during a chase scene. Fly into space and deep water without a breathing apparatus. Speak different languages without effort.

The other big difference was that rather than watching the show at home or wandering down to the local cinema to watch a blockbuster with a hundred or so others, we now absorbed the movie with 10,000 other people. It is hard to describe what it was like to watch a movie for the first time at the city cinema with such a large crowd. But let me try.

Compared to the tiny screens we were used to, the new ones were enormous. To you, Billy, these things are normal, but for us, a screen that was 160 feet high and 300 feet wide, well, that was awe-inspiring. And the sound, well, again, we were used to the "state-of-the-art" acoustics of the old movie theaters. A typical multiplex theater in the old days might have fifty speakers at best. Now we were blasted by 1,000 loudspeakers set throughout the stadium. Every person watching could hear the sound at 102 decibels, the equivalent of standing next to a chainsaw. It was mind-blowing.

If you have been to a sports event or music concert with thousands of people, you will know that at some point the crowd becomes its own organism. It moves and speaks and cheers as one. And to be part of that is truly enthralling. When a striker scores the perfect goal, or a singer hits the highest of soulful notes, it is like an electric bolt coursing through a wire. The crowd judders with the thrill of it.

So it is with watching a movie with 10,000 people. The audience reaction, their involvement, becomes part of the experience. Believe me, when that many people cry at a particularly painful plot point or laugh at an especially hilarious moment of comedy, it is truly extraordinary. Since then, the city cinemas have become even better.

Something else also happened by the end of the 2030s, Billy. You are too young to remember it, but people didn't always live together in city towers. When I was growing up, most of us lived apart. Some lived in houses in the countryside, others lived in apartments in the city. They came in all sorts of shapes and sizes. A few people had very large homes, most were smaller. Some people even lived in houseboats on rivers.

But then, starting in the early 2020s, the world was hit by a viral outbreak. This pandemic resulted in millions of deaths. The economy was massively disrupted. Sports, concerts and other cultural events were canceled. Travel was banned. As were family gatherings and funerals. The normal things in life were upended.

But then, a second pandemic struck. And then a third. Every few years, a new virus emerged, the next more powerful than the last. One started in India, another in Spain, a third in Brazil. Each time, the contagion spread around the world. In the first outbreak, people had tried to follow the rules. They mostly did what they were told. Now they rebelled. I understood, of course. How long could you expect people to stay in their separate homes under lockdown? They had to shop, they had to work, they had to see other people, the children had to go to school.

By the end of the 2020s, something had to be done, so it was decided that people should live together in enormous city towers. That way they could close the gates if a bad virus was spreading. People could then continue their lives as normal inside the city tower.

It took many years for this massive building program to be complete, but by the end of the 2030s, most of us were living in city towers. I really missed the way it used to be. How we all had our different living spaces. How we could choose when to go outdoors. But I understood the reasons, and so I became used to living inside.

19th Sept 2037

Rosemary

We last spoke a couple of years ago after Quentin's funeral.
Sorry for the too-long silence. And thank you for your
persistence. Your friendship is important to me. I really do
appreciate your efforts to provide support.

I have found it hard to speak to anyone. Please don't take it
personally. It's been four years and I still can't believe Quentin
is gone. I don't understand it. It feels like a dream. I saw his
body and I therefore know it's true.

And yet it does not feel real.

N

Nancy

8.10.37

I wish so much that I had met Quentin.
Perhaps you can tell me about him. Please.
I want to know everything. Everything.
From the start.

xx

R.

My Thoughts

I look up neoteny in Gran Nancy's dictionary. It isn't there. Another word that is new to our century. But I find juvenilization. Well, not quite. I actually see the word juvenile, which means belonging to a young person. I guess juvenilization is the process of becoming youthful. Neoteny must mean something similar.

When the dictionary was published in 1971 the word juvenile referred to teenagers. But in ancient Greece, the book says the word was used to described people between 21 and 40. Which is interesting because today a juvenile is the same age. So while our bodies might not yet be changing, it seems our words are.

I went looking for Benji. I couldn't find them anywhere. I have left them a couple of messages, no response. What if Benji tells someone about my notebook? What if that person tells the Security Control and Intelligence Police? I have written so much down that goes against the official history we are taught in school.

I have no reason to suspect that Benji is a snitch, but if there is one thing I have learned from history it's that mistakes do happen. And that things happen that are not planned. They call this "unintended consequences." My hand shakes just writing this.

I was still feeling weird when I got to school. Katia asked me what was wrong. I replied that I was worried about the math test that we were going to face in the next lesson. K didn't believe me (I never stress over math) but didn't push, instead suggesting that I take a few deep breaths. In. Out. In. Out. I tried that, but it made things worse. I got mixed up, started coughing. It made me even more panicky. K didn't give up and told me that I should count the number of breaths. One, two, three, four ... And when I reached ten, I started again at one. That helped and after a few minutes I calmed down. Which was good.

I am grateful for my friendship with K. But honestly, I would feel better if I heard from Benji.

After reading Rosemary's postcards, I hope I'll hear more about Quentin. I'm not going to push, though. *Poco a poco,* as my Spanish language bot used to say.

Gran Nancy seemed to enjoy telling me about the movies. It triggered a bunch of different memories, which led to some interesting places. Need something similar. Another form of mass entertainment. Perhaps the Olympics?

2040

I love the summer Olympic Games. I wish it could happen more often than every four years. As a child, I watched as many events as possible. The running. The swimming. The weight-lifting. The rowing.

When the spectacle came to Rome in 1960, I asked my parents to take me. But they said that at twelve years old I was too young. That it would interfere with my schoolwork. So I begged and begged, promising to do more chores, to score well at school, to attend any family event they asked. Eventually they agreed. Bless them.

I didn't mind the huge crowds or the noise. I held my father's hand tight and in we went. We took our seats and then there it was. What absolute joy. The highlight was watching Takashi Ono win three gold medals in gymnastics. He looked like he was flying as he leapt over the pommel horse. He was unstoppable! I have been hooked on the Olympic Games ever since.

The Games have changed significantly over the years. It all started with the South African sprinter and Paralympics champion Oscar Pistorius. In 2012 he became the first double-leg amputee to participate in the Olympic Games.

At the time, his running in the 400 meter was extraordinarily controversial, with many saying that his artificial limbs gave him an unfair advantage. Though he did not win a medal in the Olympics, the door was now open for other competitors to enhance their performance through technological modification.

First came the implanters. Top athletes started replacing their limbs with prosthetics. Soon they could run the 100 meter in less than nine seconds, then seven seconds, then six.

Other records were being smashed. One athlete lifted 500 kilograms, the equivalent weight of a small car. Another threw a javelin into the stadium seating area. From that point forward, the competition was taken out of the arena.

Next came the gene-changers. After it was determined that almost all premier sprinters carry the 577R genotype of ACTN3, and about a sixth of the planet did not have this gene, parents began selecting 577R for their unborn babies. Soon after, doctors identified other genes useful for sports: ones that determined endurance, strength, flexibility, recovery and tolerance to pain.

This led to a split in the world of sports. On the one hand were the Naturals, those who insisted that the only competitors allowed to participate were those who had received no technological improvements. On the other hand were the Supremes, those eager to enjoy the very best in human performance.

Then came another major change. With genetic,

prosthetic and other enrichments, women were able to compete on the same level as men. By the middle of the 2030s, the Supremes were no longer separated into male teams and female teams. This not only increased the pool of top performers — and so the quality of the games — but also provided additional entertainment. For the first time, the public saw female athletes regularly beat their male counterparts in strength and speed.

For the entire 2030s, only Naturals were eligible to take part in the Olympic Games, whilst anyone could participate in the Global Series, which was inevitably dominated by the Supremes. As the Global Series grew in popularity, the audience for the Olympics shrank. It was sad to see the Olympics lose one major sponsor and then another, and soon they were bankrupt. The solution became obvious.

Which is why this year was so exciting. Because in 2040, the Olympics was open to all competitors. No matter your enhancement or genetic upgrading. When selecting teams, what mattered now was who was the best athlete, no matter your gender or which body part you were born with. One thing remained banned. Athletes could not take performance-enhancing drugs. This was considered by the Olympics ruling body an enhancement too far.

The result was spectacular. There are too many firsts to mention, but let me give you a flavor. For the first time, a human being ran the marathon in under an hour. What an extraordinary achievement. Just twenty years earlier, the breaking of the two-hour barrier made world headlines. Then a mixed male and female team from Russia swam the 4 × 50 meter freestyle relay in 59.7 seconds, beating the much-favored Americans and becoming the first humans in history to break the minute barrier. Finally, a fifteen-year-old from Nigeria won the high jump, clearing a remarkable 16 feet — higher than a double-decker bus.

As to the future, with new and more innovative technological improvements, I imagine that these extraordinary superhuman feats are just the beginning.

15th Jan 2040

Quentin always had an opinion. He always had a sense of justice. As a child he was unbelievably argumentative. We, his father and I, said he was being rude. He said it was just that we didn't agree with him.

When he learned that his father had shaken hands with a South American dictator he was so mad he wouldn't speak to Jack for a week. At fourteen he invited three coal miners to his very conservative school. They were on strike and spoke about how the government was using the police to brutally break up their strike. He set up a debating society with his school chum Benji, who lived around the corner from us. At sixteen, they both became protestors, handing out leaflets, raising money for important causes, taking part in campaigns.

But marching and waving banners was never enough for Quentin. He and Benji had an argument. It was about tactics, I think. And from this point, Benji became interested in computers and programming while Quentin spent time in the library reading all he could about the environment and political change. He needed to make a difference.

It was always a question of logic to him. The government was not doing enough to save the world, so he had to force them to do it. He had no money, but luckily email had just been invented and he used this to link up with activists from other countries. I think these were the first people he had ever met who thought like him. They knew that the planet faced an existential crisis and they couldn't believe that nobody was doing anything about it. This was 1990!

Two years later, when he was only eighteen years old, Quentin was in Rio de Janeiro at a meeting of world leaders who gathered to discuss global warming and other environmental issues. They called this the Earth Summit. But the politicians refused to agree to the necessary changes. President George H. W. Bush said that "the American way of life is not up for negotiation."

Quentin was appalled by this inaction. He and twenty friends made fake press badges, snuck into the conference and sat down in the middle of the main hall. This sit-in caused chaos and attracted huge press interest. The protestors were picked up by Brazilian military police and arrested. This was Quentin's first taste of what he called "direct action."

I'm exhausted. Will stop there. More soon.

Nancy   17.1.40

I am so enjoying hearing about Quentin.
He sounds so amazing. Please, please
keep going. And be kind to yourself.

xx
Rosemary

Copy of Nancy's letter sent to Rosemary

23rd Jan 2040

After Rio, Quentin worked as a researcher for an environmental production company. He made one documentary about a family of polar bears, another about a venomous frog who lived in the Amazon rainforest and a third about the communication skills of the bottlenose dolphin. The films were good, really good. Quentin became a producer and then an executive producer.

But as the years went on Quentin became more and more frustrated. He said that all he was doing was making programs that attracted audiences, which helped large companies sell soap and cars and beer. That the documentaries didn't make any real difference. They celebrated wildlife, but didn't talk about how humans were destroying nature. He quit his job and became a full-time activist. He was forty-one years old.

Quentin now traveled around the UK, sleeping on people's sofas and floors, dropping into one campaign group and then another. We never knew where he was. For some reason, he found keeping in touch very difficult. Occasionally he would come home to wash his clothes, eat a good meal or get a good sleep. I was proud of him, but worried also. He seemed to be getting angrier and angrier. When he told us about his adventures, he no longer tried to entertain us with funny stories of mishaps and cock-ups. He started using words that sounded unfamiliar and cold: biocrisis, ecocide and Anthropocene.

Wanting to understand him better, I went with him to one of his meetings. Almost the entire time was spent arguing about what they called "fluffy" versus "spiky." None of it made any sense to me. Afterwards, he explained that the group had been discussing the best tactics to use. Fluffy meant raising awareness through peaceful, non-violent protest. Spiky meant destroying property and even causing physical harm to humans.

Later in the conversation he let out a long sigh as if I was dim-witted, and rattled off a long list of people who had bravely stood up against authority and changed the way we live — Nelson Mandela, Mahatma Gandhi, Umberto Sinclair, Wang Li, Claus von Stauffenberg, Malcom X, and on and on.

After it was clear that many of these names were unknown to me, he said, "It's okay, Mum, it's okay. I love you," and gave me a long hug.

Four months later, Quentin was arrested for destroying property at a laboratory where they tested beauty products on animals. After his trial and subsequent home arrest, I pleaded with him to stop. But he wouldn't listen.

Two years later, he was charged with breaking into a military base and trying to smash the nose cone of a plane capable of carrying nuclear weapons. He was given a ten-year prison sentence. Ten years for trying to stop nuclear war!

That's all for now. I need a break.

I will try and finish this letter soon.

Nancy   14.2.40

I would add some women to that list. Emmeline Pankhurst.
Marie Stopes. Anika Singh. Rosa Luxemburg. Maya Angelou.
Mary Wollstonecraft. Rosa Parks. Sarah Franklin.
More Quentin stories please.

Xx me

M 0591

Notebook 11

My Thoughts

Ecocide sounds similar to genocide and infanticide, so I'm guessing it means destruction of the ecosystem, or Earth. And bio-crisis explains itself. But I've never heard of Anthropocene. I checked my All-in-One, but it has nothing.

So I looked it up in Gran Nancy's dictionary and again, nothing.

But I did find Anthropo(s). Which is Greek for human being. And I knew from my reading about dinosaurs that a word ending with -cene means an era of Earth history. So Anthropocene must mean the period of time when humans were living on the planet. Weird to think that our species might come to an end.

Below this entry, I see a bunch of words starting with anthropo. One of them, anthropoglot, makes me laugh. Apparently, it's an animal with a tongue like a human, for instance a parrot. And just next to that was this weird one, anthropomancy, which means to tell the future by looking at people's entrails. Gross!

The dictionary says that one of the first uses of the word anthropomancy has something to do with the Roman emperor Heliogabalus. So I check out Heliogabalus on my All-in-One. And I find him. According to one ancient writer, Heliogabalus had the most unspeakably disgusting life in all history. So bad that after his death, statues and pictures of the emperor were taken down and erased. This process was called *damnatio memoriae*, or removal from memory.

Maybe that is what happened to the word Anthropocene? In 1971 when the dictionary was published the word had not yet been invented. Later it was used by Quentin and others to warn people about the SHOCK. And then, years after, someone must have removed the word from the All-in-One. But who would have done that? And why?

Could this be my first evidence that the All-in-One is monitored? Censored. Unreliable. I feel sick just writing this. Perhaps I should stop putting my thoughts down in these notebooks.

A few minutes ago something weird happened. I went looking for this notebook and couldn't find it under my mattress where I'd left it. I went in to ask Gran Nancy and saw it on the table next to the bedpod.

"Oh," Gran said. "I thought Katia put it back."

My head nearly exploded! What was K doing looking through my notebook? What pages had been seen? Apparently, K had come by again, and Gran started talking about our "little history project." After talking about it some more, Gran Nancy had said K could take a look and explained where I kept it.

"I knew you wouldn't mind," my gran said to me. "After all, those are my stories."

Benji is right. I need to be more careful about what I say and to whom. I don't want to get Gran Nancy into trouble. I don't want to get myself into trouble! Maybe I will ask her something non-political. About how society changes its taste, its likes and dislikes over time. Its fashions.

2041

Okay, happy to. Let me tell you about fashion.

For years, all anyone cared about was automation. How to deliver food, clothes, education, travel — all by machine. Then someone had the idea of turning this on its head and making a virtue of providing things not made by machine! Retro became the new trend in shopping.

The first of the retro restaurants was called Human. In a dramatic move, they announced that all their staff, including servers, hosts and even cooks, would be human, rather than robots. This was so unusual that the announcement was included in an Instanews alert.

Next came music that was delivered over the airwaves. Radio, as it used to be called, had ceased to operate more than a decade ago. But this service, free to all to use, has once again come back in style with pirate stations popping up around the world.

Soon many other brands built on this concept. You could have your hair cut or your nails trimmed by a human. A real person could read you a story. A flesh-and-blood individual could arrange your travel. You could even have your taxes done by an accountant, rather than a computer. Though the point of this I never understood. Humans are more likely to make errors.

The biggest winner of all this throwback culture was Wardrobe, the retro fashion store. This extraordinary innovation was the retail breakout success of the decade. It was a brilliant idea! First, the consumer opened an online account. Then they created their avatar by taking a 3D profile of themselves. Next, they dressed their avatar from a library' of clothes and accessories collected from more than 50 countries across 500 years. From gowns worn in seventeenth-century France to morning suits sported in Edwardian England. From colorful robes worn during the Ming Dynasty to tennis shoes peacocked in Los Angeles in the 1990s, this was a clothes wardrobe as never seen before. It must have taken years and an enormous financial investment to amass all these designs, each authentic and original to the period.

Once the article of clothing was selected, paid for and tailored to fit the customer's specific body type, it was packaged and posted to their home address. If they didn't like it, they could return it at no cost to themselves.

Unlike predictions of a fashion-less future, in which everyone walked around in the same bland clothes with the same pudding-bowl haircuts, it turns out that in reality human beings like to express themselves through their attire.

For every person who liked to wear loose-fitting clothes, there were those who preferred body-hugging apparel. While some preferred color and bedazzle, others chose muted and plain. A sizeable population liked to cover up, whilst others were moved to reveal ankles, necks, midriffs and more. And now the public could do all this not only in the fashion of today, but in the fashion of yesteryear and the year before that.

Wardrobe was a smash hit.

How did people afford all this? They still received the Dignified Income, which paid for their necessary food, transport, heating and housing, but the DI was not enough to pay for luxuries like Wardrobe.

So, people now worked as cleaners, gardeners, cooks and caretakers. Others set up workshops in their kitchens where they mended broken appliances, wrote personalized biographies and created dazzling jewelry. Others invented new and wondrous goods. I remember one year, for instance, when there was a craze for a new type of designer fruit: an apricot that grew inside a pear. Such items were, of course, sold to the mega rich.

This informal economy became known as the New Black Market. And as the years progressed, more and more people supplemented their DI with casual employment. So, within fifteen years of the Transition, many people spent their days working as before, even if they didn't need to. The supplemental income allowed them to afford additional luxuries, like a beach holiday, the latest gadget or designer clothes.

And seeing that people had found new ways of earning money, the authorities began lowering the DI. They launched a public service announcement. The one I can remember went something like "Put a smile on your face, do a little bit of work."

24th Jan 2043

In 2027, after the American prison riots, and the international
reform that followed, Quentin was released two years early.
He had changed. He spoke little. Hardly ate. He spent most
mornings in bed. Sometimes we saw the old Quentin, a
joke here or a tease there, but such moments were rare,
and served only to remind us what was lost. And then one
morning, I took a cup of tea to his room and when I opened
the door he was not there. Perhaps he had gone to the shops,
I thought, or he was seeing a friend. He didn't come back that
night or the next.

At first, I was angry, and then worried. Night after night I
cried myself to sleep. Years passed and we didn't hear from
him. Nothing. It was wretched. We had no idea what had
happened to him. Did he hate us so much that he had cut
himself off? Had he been kidnapped? Was he dead?

Then one morning three years later he turned up at our door,
just like that. He didn't even mention his absence.

"Hi, Mum," he said, giving me a hug in the kitchen where I
was cleaning the dishes, "how you been?"

I was so angry, but I didn't want him go again, so I didn't say anything.

Standing behind him was his friend Benji. It was so good to see them together. Quentin had put on some weight and seemed sunnier than before.

But when I pressed him about where he'd been, he said "around and about," gave me a wink and changed the subject. Gradually, everything returned to normal. Or what seemed like normal. We never spoke about the planet or the climate crisis that we faced. It was now obvious to all of us that urgent action was required. Cities were being evacuated. Hurricanes were causing mass destruction. The World Parliament was locked in round-the-clock emergency meetings to come up with a solution. Yet, all Quentin spoke about was the latest movie he had seen, his religious meetings with the Arborites or what I planned to make for dinner.

Then, one cold October day, Quentin was arrested again. He was charged with sending letter bombs to one of the Ethnarchs. He was now considered a "danger to society" and put in ultra-security. I was able to speak to him by phone, but never allowed to visit him. He increasingly sounded depressed. There were weeks when he refused to speak with me.

And then, two years into his sentence, I received a letter from the authorities. They said my son had died in an "accident" in prison. He was fifty-nine years old.

Later, I found out more details. They said he hanged himself from the wooden post that stuck out from the top of his bunk bed. But the post was only five feet high and Quentin was over six feet tall, so how was that possible? I wish I knew what really happened.

And now, dear friend, that's all I can do.

With kind regards,

Nancy

31.1.43

Just received your last letter 24 Jan.
People are watching my house.
I suggest extreme caution.

xxx always

My Thoughts

It has been a very long day.

It started at 4:30 a.m. with a loud knock on the door. After a while the banging stopped so I went back to sleep.

Then it started again, even louder. My bedpod was the closest so I went to see what it was. I opened the door and two Security Police officers dressed in black pushed past me.

A third one, fortyish, short and with a very thick brown beard asked gruffly, "Where's Billy Schmidt?"

For a moment I thought about lying but realized that would probably get me into more trouble.

"I'm Billy," I told the officer, who laughed and said, "I thought we was looking for a juvenile XY, this one's an XX."

I couldn't believe Bushy Beard reduced me to a chromosome! So degrading.

"Hold it!" Bushy Beard shouted to the others. "Got you!" And then lifted me up and carried me outside. Never had a chance to call out to my family. It happened too fast.

Oh, Katia — you betrayed me. How could you? I thought you were my friend!

Twenty minutes later I was being held in what they call the Pen on the fifteenth floor of our city tower. I kinda wished that I was in one of those small, quiet windowless rooms you see in the old police movies. Not like this. I was chained to a chair placed in the middle of a circular sunken space. Above me, SCIP officers were going about their noisy business. Every now and again one of them stopped by the rail and looked down on me. It made me feel extremely nervous.

Two hours later, Bushy Beard came to see me, wanting to know all about the "Old Hippie" —Benji — and how we became friends. The officer showed me the sites the Old Hippie had been browsing and the messages we had exchanged.

Luckily, I have no idea what the Old Hippie is doing. There was that strange comment about sending my notebooks back in time, but I didn't want Bushy Beard to think I was a total idiot. So I didn't mention this.

"Why are you anxious?" Bushy Beard asked me, then explained that the chair I was sitting on could read my heartbeat, blood pressure, muscular activity and perspiration rate.

Another four hours later and I was allowed to leave. This was after Bushy Beard said, "Don't forget to wave at the cameras."

Totally freaked out. Is this what people mean by a police state? In the old days, some people were scared of the police, especially because of how they often unfairly targeted racial minorities. But it's been years since the reforms, and I've always had a good experience with law enforcement. If this is happening to me, how do they treat people who really don't like Ethnarchs?

Need to tell Benji but not sure how to contact them without being monitored. Also, I realize that my notebooks could cause me real trouble if found. Two options. First, destroy them. But it's taken so much work and I feel I would be letting down Gran Nancy. So, second, hide them somewhere safe. I have a couple of good ideas.

I've also been thinking more about the postcards and letters Gran Nancy gave me. They just make things more confusing. Did Quentin die in an accident or not? I've tried asking a few times, but it has become clear that Gran Nancy doesn't want to speak any more about this. Not sure if I should feel angry or sad. Could the Security Police really have killed Quentin? I can't believe it. But what if they did ...?

And what was that about Quentin and the Arborites? I asked my parents, but they told me to mind my own business and quickly changed the subject.

I must remember to ask Gran Nancy next time we speak.

2045

The Arborites were a religious group. Well, something like that. They were also environmentalists. I don't like talking about religion. It has been the cause of countless misunderstandings, numerous wars, so much guilt and self-doubt. Religion makes me feel profoundly anxious. It is filled with so many words, and each comes with its own long and complicated history.

Its people: priests, rabbis, imams, disciples, messiahs, archangels, gods and prophets.

Its practices: prayer, fasting, recitation, meditation, self-flagellation.

Its ceremonies and rites of passage: circumcisions, christenings, baptisms, confirmations, weddings and funerals.

Its places: heaven, hell, paradise, land of milk and honey.

Its books: the Koran, Bible, Torah, Vedas, Tripitaka, Book of Mormon.

And these are just a few words from just a few of the religions!

Most of all, I struggle with the suspension of rational

thought. As a historian, one who writes about deeds and actions with care and precision, it seems to me that religion defies logic. How can one speak about fact and truth, and therefore history, when talking about faith and belief — and perhaps even miracles? I don't think you can.

Yet, despite my personal reservations, and despite (or maybe because of) society's increasing reliance on science and technology, religion has grown ever stronger. So, you are right, Billy, to ask about this part of our collective history. To avoid it would be a gross omission. I will, however, tread carefully on this topic. Let me start with the facts.

In the years after the SHOCK there was a massive boom in the world's biggest religions. More than 70 percent of the global population said they belonged to one religious group or another. As the planetary catastrophe worsened, people increasingly looked to faith and spirituality for answers and comfort. Of course, that left 30 percent who were not religious. Who did not look to God or a priest for guidance or relief. But they belonged to a shrinking minority.

As the crisis worsened, more and more people joined the mainstream religions. Two religions that benefited particularly were Christianity and Judaism. After all, the apocalypse was clearly predicted in the Hebrew and Christian scriptures — plagues of locusts, earthquakes, floods, terrible winds and famines.

What was notable was that these new followers were fundamentalists. They believed in the literal interpretation of the ancient books. They believed in the old laws. The unequal treatment of men and women. Intolerance of homosexuality. And, most of all, an eye for an eye. If you transgressed the law, you experienced terrible and immediate retribution.

It made me sad, though, when they ended Christmas. Why did they do this? Because the fundamentalists said that Christmas was based on a pagan holiday, which to be factual, it was. They also didn't like how the festival had become all about consumerism, which was of course frowned upon after the SHOCK. Moreover, they said it was unlikely Jesus was born in winter because (according to their Bible) at the time of his birth, shepherds were out with their flocks in the fields for the springtime lambing season. Finally, they said that Jesus didn't even celebrate his birthday, so we should follow his example.

As a child, I loved having a Christmas tree in our house. We spent hours dressing it with sparkling balls and strings of colorful beads. On Christmas Eve, we left out a plate of biscuits by the fireplace for Father Christmas and a carrot for Rudolph, his trusty reindeer. Then, on Christmas morning, my siblings and I ran down to see what presents were under the tree. But in all but a few homes, this has long gone. The one thing I don't miss are the endless Christmas songs they always used to play in the stores, over and over again, starting in early November.

Islam also grew rapidly. But unlike the increasingly conservative path pursued by the Christians and Jews, Muslims focused on public service and inclusivity. They provided support to victims of flooding, poverty and climate trauma. They supported same-sex marriage and women leading prayers in mosques. This community-centered approach attracted tens of millions of new followers to Islam.

But the SHOCK also ushered in a new religion: Arborism. And this was the group that Quentin belonged to.

The Arborites believed in nature, in science, in the redemptive power of the non-human universe. Their great fear was not the loss of God's love or the inability to enter heaven but the destruction of Planet Earth. For them, the apocalypse was the ruin of the natural world by humans: climate change, the devastation of the coral reefs and the rainforests, biological warfare, nuclear meltdowns. Greed, consumerism and waste — these were their great vices. Large corporations, army chiefs and heads of governments were their demons, jinns and Antichrists.

The Arborites worshipped the natural world and, in particular, trees, which were some of the planet's oldest inhabitants. Their meetings took place in ancient woodlands and tropical rainforests. In small copses surrounded by fields of wildflowers and thick groves overlooking the sea. These were joyous, loud and happy affairs. More like music festivals than religious services.

Their "book" was not the Koran or Bible or Bhagavad Gita. Instead it was the biosphere, the genetic manuscript upon which all life was written. Their prophets were Charles Darwin, James Lovelock, Rachel Carson, Al Gore,

Petra Kelly, Vandana Shiva, Wangari Maathai and Katia Zhao. And inspired by the Ten Commandants from the Jewish Torah, the Arborites had eight commandments:

1. Do not kill (humans or other animals).
2. Honor and respect Mother Earth above all else.
3. Leave no trace.
4. Live within your means.
5. Maintain biodiversity.
6. Do not pollute.
7. Do not lie.
8. Share the planet's resources equitably with all other beings.

This new religion became so popular with the younger generation that some of the leaders of the older faiths worried about their future. They adopted some of the Arborite creed, especially their love of nature and respect for animals. They used some of the most popular rituals. Church services were now held outside in fields. Hindu weddings took place in the forest.

But the Arborites' call for putting the survival of the planet before the survival of humans worried the Ethnarchs even more. They said that the meetings were not about religion or spirituality or compassion for non-human animals. Instead, they said Arborite meetings attracted troublemakers and were an opportunity to agitate against society. Supporters of the Ethnarchs questioned the Arborites' patriotism and loyalty. They declared that you were either with us, or against us. That if you belonged to an Arborite congregation, then you were a traitor to the species.

So the Ethnarchs approved laws making it illegal to attend Arborite gatherings. And if you were found guilty of providing an Arborite with money, food or any other kind of support, you were arrested.

We no longer saw the happy, large, open-air gatherings we had become used to. The Arborites were driven underground. Meetings were held in secret. Communications were made by code. And if they were not been so before, the Arborites were now very political.

Quentin and his friends plotted and schemed and organized. They saw themselves as defenders of the planet. And the Ethnarchs saw them as enemies of the new world order.

More laws were passed cracking down on the Arborites. Surveillance increased. You never knew whether the person you were speaking with was a SCIP informant. Employers were asked to investigate their employees. If they were found to have knowledge that their staff were Arborites then they, the bosses, could be arrested for failure to report illegal activity.

It was a terrible time.

From: Daniel Humphries <DH242@cam.ac.uk>
Subject: Meeting request
Date: September 11, 2045 at 8:06:29 PM GMT+1
To: Nancy Schmidt <NS998@cam.ac.uk >

Dear Professor Schmidt,

Please make yourself available for a little chat on Wednesday at 5 o'clock. Bring copies of every paper, letter and other document you have produced in the past three years. The topic for discussion is the difference between the right kind of history and the wrong kind of history.

Yours,

Master Humphries

12.12.45.

Roses are sed
Violets are blue.

There are facts that are said,

And facts that are true.

My Thoughts

I don't know what to make of our conversation on religion. Most of my friends attend a church, mosque or synagogue. I've been to a few services myself. The last one took place in the bio-field about two hours' walk from our home. I liked it. The beautiful surroundings. The songs with their catchy tunes. The feeling of being together. In fact, I may see if I can find another gathering to attend in the next few days. But I had no idea that they banned this other religion, Arborism. I've never heard of it. And there is no mention of it in my All-in-One.

As to Father Christmas, that's a really strange one. Why would adults make up a story about a large red-suited man with a white beard who breaks into your house every year? And then reinforce this story by saying this old man gives children presents? I would have thought it would be hard to encourage children to tell the truth in this context.

Hold on! Beginning to think that's what's happened to me. I've been told a fake story all these years. About a group of kind old fellows who have nice things delivered to my door? Also known as "The Ethnarchs."

And how about that letter from Gran Nancy's boss at

Cambridge about "the right kind of history"? Why was this Master Humphries requesting to see letters and documents? Was Gran Nancy being monitored? And why share this with me? It felt like Gran Nancy was sending me a message: you're not alone, we are in this together, stay strong.

I was walking toward the gym today when I saw Katia going into the gym about one hundred feet away. I sprinted forward. I wanted to say that I feel betrayed. That I'm angry. That my family is now in danger. But by the time I reached the door it had closed. I pulled at it, but it was locked. I banged hard on the glass, yelling, "Katia, Katia, Katia!" But my words were lost. K continued down the corridor, turned right and into the changing rooms. As if nothing was the matter.

Notebook 13

My Thoughts

Something happened when I got home just now.

I found Gran Nancy sleeping in the bedpod. Gran looks really ill these days. More cold gray than the normal warm brown. Eating almost nothing. Drinking even less. The one thing Gran likes is frozen juice bars, so I make sure there are plenty around.

I leaned down to kiss Gran and saw a card sticking out of an old book next to the pillow. I pulled it out and read it. It said:

"If Benji comes to the house call us."

There was also a number written down.

I went into our kitchen and called the number on the card. The automated answering service said: "You have reached the Security Control and Intelligence Police. Press 1 to speak to the officer on duty ..." Before it got to number two I hung up.

Twenty seconds later I was back with Gran Nancy. I was out of breath. And I was desperate to understand what is going on.

I shook my gran awake. Gran Nancy's eyes opened and I pressed record on my All-in-One.

2047

Give me a moment to wake up. Okay. Okay. That's better. Let me try and explain.

Quentin would not have died, if he was not in prison. He would not be in prison, if it was not for his political activities. And he would not be involved with politics, if it was not for his "friend" Benji. Benji has been a menace to this family. A menace to society …

Hold on. Hold on. Before you go asking a thousand questions. You came to me with this idea about recording my history. At first, I went along with it, thinking it was cute. And anyway, what harm could come of talking about the old days? Perhaps I could teach you a few things. Pass on a little wisdom. But then I heard from the Security Police that Benji was talking to you as well. That you were meeting in secret. I was not going to allow that. I wasn't going to lose another child. Not because of Benji.

No, no, no! This is not your turn to speak. You need to listen to me. Hear me out. When we started these conversations, you promised to listen to me and to write down what I said verbatim. Will you break your bond? No? Good. Then let me continue.

I reached out to SCIP. And they said they had an active investigation against Benji. That he was a troublemaker ... Okay, sorry. That "they" were a troublemaker. You must remember, I am an old woman. It's hard for me to remember the right words to say all the time.

Anyway, the Security Police said that he, they, were a threat to peace and the order of things. A hooligan.

Well, I couldn't disagree with that. SCIP said they had been trying to arrest them for months, but they kept slipping away. Never in the same place for more than one night. No presence on the One/Net. No real friends or associates to speak of. SCIP asked me to help. And so I did. Because I believe in the rule of law. I believe the Security Police is a force for good. That without them, our community would collapse into chaos. They have my full support.

We always thought that the future would be a police state. Well, at least I did. Perhaps I had read too many science fiction novels written in the sad, dark years after the mass tragedy of the Second World War. From these stories, I saw a life strictly controlled by a faceless authority, harsh rules that would restrict my day-to-day life and that would be enforced by brutal, mirthless jackboots. I imagined that my friends and neighbors who broke these rules would disappear during the night, that the world would be full of grays and muted colors, that humor and creativity would be replaced by uniformity, isolation and boredom.

Instead, things are more exciting, more varied, more

creative, more colorful and, on the whole, I would say far happier than I anticipated.

Sure, there is a security force that does impose law and order. And the punishment for infraction is both immediate and severe. Home imprisonment, zero communication with the outside world, enormous fines that take years to repay and worst of all, boredom.

And yes, the political system is not as free as it used to be. By "free," I really mean chaotic. Back in the day, when I was far younger, I was told that my vote counted. So, each election day I dutifully went to my neighborhood polling station, put an X next to the candidate I preferred — though in truth I typically just voted for the party that I had voted for all my life — and cast my ballot …

Hang on, I am not done yet. Let me finish what I am saying …

Be patient, Billy. This is important. I know you have a lot to say. You always say how curious you are, that you love history. Well, okay, then listen.

About thirty years ago, there came the populist revolutions. In a short space of time, a new breed of politicians swept to power across the world. These politicians were funny, eccentric, loud and provocative, but they had never held power before. They were entertainers, performers, showmen and show-women, One/Netters, beauty queens and talk-show hosts.

Yet they were elected, fairly and without fraud or corruption. And when they took hold of the reins of government, they made an absolute mess. One after the other, they undermined decades of hard-fought regulations. Laws that defended the weak and safeguarded the innocent. Laws that protected the planet and the fragile environment in which we live. Laws that prevented the country from making stupid mistakes, like printing money when they wanted to build themselves a new highway, or wall or power plant. Or starting a war against an enemy they could not beat.

Something, it seemed, had happened to the voters. After a century of women having the right to vote — a right that was won despite tremendous pain and suffering — the people just didn't seem to care anymore. It was as if the entire planet seemed to collectively shrug its shoulders and declare, "No matter who we vote for, our lives don't seem to improve so we might as well vote for someone who entertains us."

And after it became absolutely plain that the populists who were elected to run our governments were making things far, far worse, it was decided that democracy, such as it was, had to be abandoned.

Who made this decision? This was less clear. Certainly it was not the politicians themselves, for they would never have chosen to lose power. Just like the turkeys, back in the days of meat-eating, would never have voted in favor of Thanksgiving dinner.

And just as certainly, it was not the people, the voters, the great heaving masses, for why would they have given up the right to select their decision-makers, even if these very same decision-makers were making their lives worse, year after year after year.

At the time nothing was clear. We guessed that probably, if it was anyone, it was the hidden elites. Those mysterious brokers who controlled the levers of power. They spoke to the right people and opened the right doors. And before any of us knew what had happened, we had a new political system. Centralized, consolidated, coordinated, supranational and very much out of our hands.

As the years went by, it became obvious to everyone, even the most dim-witted, that the new system worked far better than the old. With a growing agreement that life was better, the shadow lifted, and the true masters were revealed.

What had happened was this. The CEOs of the top hundred companies in the world had taken over. They decided that they knew best — and by the way, they were right — so in the interest of the many, the few would now be in charge.

Of course, we were told we still had a say in our lives. Indeed, they said we had even more control, that sovereignty had been taken from the failed governments and returned to us, the people.

The truth was quite different. For though we were consulted from time to time on the big issues of the day through referenda — Should we keep the death penalty? Should we make abortion available to all? Should meat be abolished? — the supreme executives who now ran things, the technocrats and bureaucrats, the policy wonks and bean-counters, the geeks and the nerds, they were the real ones who were making the decisions.

They called themselves the Ethnarchs. To me that seemed an unnecessary reference to a bygone era. Perhaps that was the point. To reassure us that change had happened before, so all would be well with the world.

I don't know how the Ethnarchs organized themselves. I often wondered if they met in person or only communicated by the One/Net. Their inner operations were shrouded in secrecy, obscure, beyond the view of the general public.

We were told that there was no leader, that they shared a community of interests, that they made their decisions by consensus. If two or more disagreed with a decision, then it was rejected. They said that all decisions were based on the very latest and best research and analysis available. This was the foundation of their power: Mega Data. The suggestion was that they had the information, we did not, so let them get on with making the decisions. Their slogan was: Power is information. Their mantra was TINA — There Is No Alternative. As far as the Ethnarchs were concerned, public consent was irrelevant.

At the very beginning, there were a few who protested and campaigned against the Ethnarchs. Who said that voting was a human right, that without democracy, the powerful would abuse the less fortunate. Who argued that we had entered into a new autocracy, in which the corporate elite were our new slave masters. These radicals were joined by the bloated populists who were out of power. But nobody cared about those losers. For years, they had screamed that immigrants, the media, the judges and the courts were their enemies. They had complained too many times and made things far worse.

So I didn't listen to them. Nor did anyone else. After all, things were better, so what did it matter?

If it hadn't been for the SHOCK, maybe then I would have fought more for democracy. But our environment was in crisis, our planet was in real peril. You don't remember what it was like. For a while it was touch and go. We almost lost everything. Giving up a little power was the least I could do to ensure the survival of our species.

Don't look at me like that. Like I have deceived you.

I was protecting you.

Protecting our family.

That's why I worked with the Security Police. For a good reason. I didn't get anything out of it. They didn't pay me. You are just a youngster. You don't understand these things. SCIP is there to look after us. I know they can be frightening. But they are one of the consequences we have to live with, because of the terrible mistakes that we made in the past.

I am sorry for this. I wish that we had done more to stop the SHOCK from happening. I wish we didn't have the Ethnarchs and the Security Police. I wish we could travel more and have more freedom. I wish we didn't have to choose between security on the one hand and freedom on the other. But that's where we are. What's done is done. We can't change the past, but we can change the future.

Hey, Billy, don't walk out on me!

And by the way, you never asked my permission to give the history to Benji. You never said you planned to share my memories with other people.

Come back. Billy, please ...

My Thoughts

It was at that point that I walked out of the room. I just couldn't take it anymore. Gran Nancy lecturing me on and on about the past. Not giving me a chance to speak. Sure, I agreed to take down every sentence, every paragraph, word for word. But really. We're way past our little history project now.

And I can't believe Gran Nancy is fine with a police state. Fine with putting people in custody without charge. Tying them to a chair and keeping them for hours while they are questioned.

I don't know what makes me feel worse. That it was Gran Nancy who betrayed me. Gran Nancy. My own relative. Or that I've been played. I've been so naive! I thought I was having a good old time talking about the past and learning a few things from my elders. Turns out I was just some ignorant pawn in a game of four-dimensional chess. What a fool I've been!

I'm so, so sorry, Katia, for not trusting you. I've been a terrible friend.

Well, if Gran Nancy and those SCIP buffoons think I can be scared off easily, they've got another thing coming.

I grabbed one of my parent's old coats, a thick hat and a pair of old glasses, and went out. I had to find Benji.

I visited the Good Juice Bar where we first met. Not there.

To their gym. Nothing.

Their old place of Community. No sign of Benji there either.

I spent the whole night looking. On and on, asking if anyone had seen Benji. There wasn't a trace of them anywhere.

It was around six in the morning when I headed home. Exhausted and defeated. What was I going to say to my parents? They would be worried sick wondering where I was all night. And what am I going to say to Gran Nancy? Will we ever be able to look into each other's eyes again without a sense of pain?

I turned the final corner and glanced toward our front door. And there they were. Benji, a dark hood covering their head, a long piece of string flipping between their palms. Waiting for me.

A few minutes later we were crouched in a dark corridor behind the cantina my family usually eats in. I figured they wouldn't have cameras there.

"I've cracked it," said Benji excitedly.

That made me happy and I asked them to show me Two Coyotes Running Apart.

"No not that!" they said like I was an idiot. "I've found a way to send your notebooks back. In time."

So I hadn't misheard them.

Benji said they had invented an algorithm. Something about data compression and wormholes. And they'd managed to hack into a quantum computer. Not sure which one. I really don't understand any of it. They were speaking so fast. Benji looked worked up. Eyes massively dilated. Did I still want to do it?

It didn't take me long to decide. If people in the past read my notebooks, then they would know that they have to act. Because if they don't, the consequences would be devastating. And they would know that. Right?

But I know we have a problem. How will the people in the past know that these notebooks are real? Won't they, like me, think that time travel is fantasy? Just science fiction?

I thought and thought about this. All the while Benji was fidgeting nervously. They couldn't sit still. Flicking the string between their fingers. This way and that. Over and over. Muttering at me, "Hurry up. Hurry up."

Then it came to me. In a kidnap situation, the hostage-taker provides a "proof of life," evidence that their victim is still alive. A photograph of them holding that day's news-paper — or at least that's what I've seen in my favorite detective show from the 2010s. Surely the equivalent would be to write events that were just about to happen to the readers in their near future. That would convince them.

The trick will be to send the history back to a date that gives enough time to stop the SHOCK from happening, but close enough that inaction will feel scary. We agree 2020 would be best.

Benji said they can't select a specific day or week, but perhaps they can narrow it down to a month. "More or less."

"What about where it goes?" I asked.

Benji thought about this. "That article your gran gave you, which newspaper was it from?"

"The *Guardian*," I said.

"Okay, let's send it there. Presumably they have people there who care about the environment." We looked at the article, which I'd tucked in the second notebook, and found the newspaper's address on the bottom of the page.

This does not give me much confidence, but it's the best plan we have. The only plan we have.

Benji and I agreed to meet in two hours at the same spot. If I don't come back, they will send the second notebook they already have.

And then it happened, just as I was getting up to leave.

"Oh, my goodness!" Benji said.

I turned around to take a look. There between Benji's fingers were two triangles, each with a tail.

"Those are the two coyotes," they said.

And then slowly, as if by magic, the two coyotes moved along the string, away from each other. They pulled apart. Benji did it!

When I arrived home, the light in my parents' pod was off. So was the one in Gran Nancy's room. I collected my notebooks from the hiding place.

That was a minute ago.

This is now.

I am sitting at our kitchen table. The notebooks are stacked in a pile next to me.

And this is the plan. As notebook number 13 is almost full, I'm going to start a new one and add a long list of facts from my All-in-One. I'll label it number 14.

I'm going to add a bunch of facts for the year 2022 (just two years ahead of the year we're sending the notebooks back to), so whoever finds them has proof that they really do come from the future. Just for starters, I'm thinking about:

Winner of the men's football World Cup
Winner of the women's single bobsleigh at the winter
    Olympics
The number of seats won at the United States
    Congress midterm election
The hottest day of the year for five capital cities
The lowest point for the Nikkei stock market
The winner of the Prix de l'Arc de Triomphe
    horse race
The winner of the Tokyo Marathon

That kind of thing. Facts from all over the world. If nothing else, whoever finds this information can make a fortune on the betting markets. Time to get to work.

It's now half an hour later. I've filled fifteen pages in notebook number 14. I've only got thirty minutes. I don't want to be late for Benji. I'm going to go now —

No, wait.

I'm still angry at Gran Nancy. But I feel like we need to talk. Now, before it's too late. Besides, it doesn't feel right to end the history on my last conversation with Gran Nancy. With bad feelings left on the page.

There is just enough room in the 13th notebook to add a few more words, so I'll take it with me. I want to end things right.

I knocked on the door and went in.

Gran Nancy could barely speak. Words came out as little more than a whisper.

After a pause, I said that I understood that my gran has been trying to look after me and the family. That my heart is full of respect and admiration. And that, more than anything, I love my Gran Nancy.

At that, my gran smiled and squeezed my hand.

I have one more topic, I said. I leaned in, so close I could feel Gran Nancy's breath on my cheek, and asked my question.

2050

My dear, dear Billy, I am feeling so tired, but you have asked about the future. I am afraid that I do not think there is much of a future for me. But I have had a long life so there is nothing to be sad about. I am grateful for all that I have had. And even though there have been losses and regrets, I have had a good life.

As a historian, of course, I cannot know for sure what will happen in years to come. For how can one speak with certainty about events that are still to happen?

And yet, and yet.

As you know, even historians — who declare that their entire worldview is based on facts and objective truths, built upon the solid foundations of hard evidence, robust documentation and irrefutable testimony — accept that past events are at best subject to interpretation and at worst entirely up for debate. It is not without reason that people say that history is written by the victors, precisely because the official record depends on who tells it.

More than this, it has been my experience that it is possible to say that certain things in the future are highly likely to happen. Perhaps even more than likely — obvious.

Let me give you some examples.

In the 1930s, it was clear to almost anyone who read the papers that war was coming. Which is why countries like Germany, England, Japan and France spent so much money investing in building their military forces years ahead of the outbreak of the Second World War.

Equally, in the 1950s, much was clear about the years to come. Women would play a more equal role at home and at work. More people would own refrigerators, drive cars, speak by phone. People would live for longer as vaccination programs and health services improved around the world.

The same was true in the 1990s. For those who experienced the early days of the One/Net, it was clear that this was a new utility, likely to spread fast and wide, as important as electricity or clean water. Mass automation would soon be upon us, revolutionizing the way we worked and spent our leisure time. And despite centuries of intolerance, once it had started it was clear that more and more countries around the world would allow people to marry regardless of sexual orientation. Because who wants to stop two people celebrating their love?

And again and again and again, one truth has been repeated. Human societies are riddled with problems and issues and existential threats, and it is only through the determined, courageous actions of a small number of individuals and groups that progress is achieved. Progress that is necessary for human survival and human happiness.

If we can say, therefore, that historical truth is between

75 and 80 percent accurate — which as a historian I would say is being generous — can we not say the same about future truth? In other words, both are based on facts and both require a degree of interpretation?

I have tried my best to tell the history of the past thirty or so years, fifteen years before you were born, and then during your life. And now we have reached the year 2050. Let me add one more note. The most important note —

Life is good. Despite all the hardships and crisis, both for society and on a personal level, we live in a time of safety and calm.

Today there are now over 11 billion people living in the world, and most of us live in cities. On average a child born today can expect to live for more than a century. Their life will be one of ease and comfort compared to a hundred years ago.

There are problems of course. When are there not? Perhaps the worst is inequality. Whilst everyone is guaranteed a Dignified Income, a house, education, health care and a leisure occupation that will fulfill them, those at the top of society have extraordinary wealth.

This would be bad enough if it were a little-known fact, but for reasons that I have never understood, the most powerful amongst us like to boast about their extravagant lifestyles. The media is forever filled with shows cataloging one celebrity or another's newest expensive toy, or home, or adventure. This fosters resentment and anger amongst many.

And sadly, many of the old injustices exist. For while

the DI has assured a substantial basic income for everyone, racism and inequality remain. An Ethnarch is still most likely to be a White man. There is more wealth in countries like Germany, China and the US than in Sudan, Nepal or Chile. Women still suffer domestic violence. And strangers — whether they be from another town or another country — are often treated with fear and mistrust.

In general, however, for almost everyone, things are better. This is a time of optimism and well-being. As a historian, I of course know that this can change overnight, with astonishing speed and force. There are plenty of examples over the past three or four hundred years where complacency and naivety have been suddenly overcome by tyranny and oppression. The phrase "we must not forget" must not be forgotten.

But, as I have said, for the vast, vast majority life is good. Certainly better than it was when I was younger. And one of the things I have learned in life is to appreciate the good things. The cloudless days. The quiet walks in the woods. The amusing story told by a friend. The happy coincidence. The tasty meal. The night of calm and restful sleep.

Because, within a twinkle of an eye, the good things can be gone.

My Thoughts

I quickly jotted down what Gran Nancy said — I'm so glad we spoke — and now I'm back with Benji. In the alley.

And now, as I write these final words, Benji is telling me to hurry. We must act fast. The Security Police could come at any time.

I have given Benji everything. All the notebooks. So these are my final words.

If anyone does read this "future history," please understand that it is only one of your possible futures.

So please change your behavior. Now.

Change society's behavior. So that the SHOCK never happens.

Because if you don't —

It will be catastrophic for me and my friends and my family.

It will be catastrophic for your descendants and your friends' descendants.

It will be catastrophic for the planet.

Please, please, please, choose wisely.

Protect your future.
Protect our present.
Before it's too late.

Billy Schmidt
15 June 2050

Epilogue from the researcher

Those were the final few words written down at the back of the last notebook.

How these notebooks arrived here, in the Berlin archive, is a mystery. Especially after reading that Benji's intention had been to send them back to the Guardian in London.

I looked through the box again to see if I could find the notebook Billy mentioned with all the facts from 2022, the one titled "14." It was missing.

As were numbers 3, 5, 8 and 12.

I have no idea how these notebooks could have got lost, but then again, I have no idea how any of the notebooks came to be here in 2020.

I read through the notebooks again, and then a third time. As I went along, I took detailed notes, trying to make sense of it. Most of all, I was struck by the mundanity of the horror, how the difficulties brought about by the Climate SHOCK had been normalized, accepted.

On my fourth go-through, I was hit by what Billy said — that this was only one possible future. Perhaps we could call it an alternate future.

And if this was right, then why couldn't we choose a different path? One that would entail difficult choices for sure, but would result in a vastly improved outcome for all of us.

Which is why I am publishing this now. Hopefully you, the reader, will do as Billy implores: choose wisely before it's too late.

Thomas Harding
Researcher

Glossary

577R – genotype of ACTN3
ACTN3 – gene linked to sprinters
All-in-One – electronic device
Arborites – environmental religious group
Bedpod – where people sleep
DI – Dignified Income, basic income for everyone
E3 – end-to-end-to-end encryption
ENASO – European and North American Security Organization
Ethnarchs – business people who run the world
FDP – Full Data Protection
Gene-changers – people who select genes during surrogacy
Globals – international currency
Global Series – open athletic games dominated by Supremes
Implanters – athletes who replaced their limbs with prosthetics
Insta-ice – popular frozen desert
Instanews – major source of news
IPCC – International Panel on Climate Change
iShelf – application that stores digital books
Mega Data – data collected by Quantum Computers

Megas – the wealthiest of the wealthy

MoonBase1 – colony on the Moon

Naturals – athletes who compete without enhanced body parts

One/Net – formerly known as the internet

Populists – politicians who told voters what they wanted to hear

Quantum supremacy – the moment when a quantum computer could perform a task that a traditional computer could not

SCIP – Security Police

SHOCK – the moment of climate change crisis

Supremes – the very best of the Implanters

TOBS – The One in a Billions, the wealthiest of the wealthy

Transition – the time during which most jobs were automated and many people stopped working

UN – United Nations

Warbot – autonomous armed drone

WP – World Parliament

WTO – World Trade Organization

THOMAS HARDING is a bestselling author whose books have been translated into more than sixteen languages. His books include *Hanns and Rudolf*, which won the JQ-Wingate Prize for Non-Fiction; *The House by the Lake*, which was shortlisted for the Costa Biography Award, and which was adapted into a picture book; and *Blood on the Page*, which won the Crime Writers' Association Golden Dagger Award for Non-Fiction. Thomas lives in Hampshire, England.